"I warmly endorse the continuing efforts of Dan Woll and Walter Rhein for their latest novel, "Paperclip." Unsettled, stirring. drama-laden—

"Paperclip" is written with gusto, good humor and a knowledge of the panoply that is America, as the authors take their three gifted characters from youth to adulthood. How can you resist a book that opens with a guesser who is always right? "Paperclip" begs for a read, a sequel, and a movie."

—Dave Wood

Former Books Editor, *Minneapolis Star Tribune*,

Past Vice-President, *National Book Critics Circle*

Paperclip

DAN WOLL
&
WALTER RHEIN

Burning Bulb
PUBLISHING

Paperclip
By **Dan Woll & Walter Rhein**

Burning Bulb Publishing
P.O. Box 4721
Bridgeport, WV 26330-4721
United States of America
www.BurningBulbPublishing.com

Cover illustration by Walter Rhein.
Edited by Cas Peace

First Edition.

Paperback Edition ISBN: 978-1-948278-08-9

Printed in the United States of America

CHAPTER 1

Blue Ribbon

There was strength in how she stood defiant, but not enough to disguise her inherent vulnerability. The young girl wore a white spring dress with green embroidery over the heart and a blue ribbon in her hair. Twelve years old, she still had the elfin-like build of a small child. Throughout her neighborhood she was known to be polite and kind. An air of joy surrounded her and her presence brightened any gathering. Strangers felt a pull to assist her in moments of distress. Unfortunately, at that moment, the street was empty save for one dark figure and his creature.

Before her stood a snarling beast. The animal was a savage German Shepherd, with feral muscles rippling under greasy hair. Time slowed for the girl as the beast focused its considerable blood lust upon her. The dog's ears peeled back, its hackles raised. Ridges formed in its face, and teeth flashed beneath curled lips. Worst of all, its eyes shone like lasers; bloodshot red, they bored deep into the girl's soul and reflected no hint of mercy or compassion.

Next to the dog the stranger stood with long hair protruding from beneath a black Stetson hat like strands of a soiled mop. A self-satisfied smirk was plastered across his face and he seemed to draw pleasure from beholding the girl's terror. He waited, neither commanding the dog to attack nor to heel; savoring the moment, fixated on the girl's terrified trembles.

The cowboy stood over six feet tall, thin with hard muscle. Darkness emanated from him. The girl could sense something beyond the lurking rot of a corrupt adult. She often saw things others could not, things that existed on a plain of reality between sleep and consciousness. Through the filter of her special vision, midnight smoke billowed from the sockets of the cowboy's eyes.

The cowboy had moved into a rental property a few houses down two weeks before and appeared to have a supernatural awareness of the exact places and times when he could find her alone. She realized now he'd been scouting before. This time was different.

"I like your blue ribbon," the cowboy said. "My mother used to wear a ribbon like that."

The girl, Carlie, did not reply.

"Is this you?" the cowboy asked with a menacing drawl. He lifted up the newspaper clipping he was clutching.

Carlie stood her ground even as the dog began to lunge in her direction again and again. She was on her way home from St. Asors. The nuns had told her not to talk to strangers, but they'd never given any practical advice about a situation like this. The beast's repugnant breath produced a foul cloud that polluted the air and addled her thinking. The cowboy brandished the clipping. Even at a distance, Carlie recognized the image. She wished not to respond, but felt her head dip in an involuntary nod. The intrusion on Carlie's psyche awakened a defense she didn't know she had.

"Ahhhh," the stranger replied, but then he paused, noticing the determined look that crossed Carlie's face. Before he could explore the subtle change, a man's angry voice interrupted them.

"What's going on here?"

Carlie felt something snap in her mind, and only then was she able to take a step back, away from the snarling animal. The voice belonged to her dad, Alan, but her newfound power came from within. Instinctively, she focused on a tingling electric feeling in her chest until it felt as if she were forming a psychic shield. The stranger seemed to sense it too, and he backed off as if he had been shocked. Just then her dad came charging across the lawn in a state halfway between hysteria and rage.

"Sorry, pod'ner," the cowboy said, turning his attention to the man and surreptitiously folding the clipping into a wad which he shoved into his back pocket. "I apologize for the behavior of ol' Scorpio. He's a bit excitable. But it is a public sidewalk."

The cowboy seemed to deflate. To Carlie's perspective, he condensed down from a spectral creature wreathed in smoke to the less intimidating form of a lanky street dweller. Cowed, the cowboy turned to go, yanking hard on Scorpio's leash. Carlie noticed he had a limp and wore a funny fat shoe that protruded beneath the cuff of his bell bottoms.

"I've seen you around before," Carlie's dad stated, his brow furrowed in fruitless concentration. Carlie watched her dad try to push through some obvious discomfort, but something seemed to block him from completing his thought. Carlie instinctively recognized that the cowboy was exerting his power. Frustrated, her dad changed tactics. "You leave now. I am calling the police. Your dog is never to bother my girl again."

Offering a weak smirk, the cowboy cast a final glance at Carlie. If he'd intended to instill one final dose of intimidation, he'd miscalculated. Carlie was shy; her parents were working with her to look people in the eye. This was the last person for whom they'd intended that lesson to apply, but something made Carlie look up. Her eyes fused with those of the stranger. With a jolt of pure willpower, she sent the energy gathering within her breast into an assault on the dark stranger. She couldn't be entirely sure if her humiliation and fear had deluded her into playing games, but she felt a primordial need to respond to the threat he represented. A shock went through her body like touching the sparkplug on a lawn mower, and Carlie was surprised to see the cowboy flinch.

The hound picked that moment to lunge again, and this time the beast took its owner by surprise. The jaws flashed, but Carlie recoiled and the salivating maw snapped shut inches from her cheek.

"Get that monster out of here!" her dad howled. He stepped forward to pull Carlie behind him and kicked the dog as the cowboy grabbed the snarling monster by his spiked collar. The cowboy lumbered away without looking back as Carlie's dad pulled his little girl to the house, slammed the door, and then knelt before her to inspect for injuries.

"Did he bite you?" he said, trembling all over.

"No Dad, I'm fine."

"Did he bite you, did he bite you?" her dad continued, becoming frantic as he checked her.

"Dad, I'm fine!" Carlie replied, then resorted to the trick she'd seen her mom use. "Alan, it's OK!"

At the invocation of his name, her dad returned to himself and enveloped Carlie in a warm hug.

"I'm sorry, honey, I'm sorry." He embraced Carlie, then held her away to look her in the eyes. "Stay away from that man, do you hear me?"

"Yes."

"Promise me you'll stay away."

"I promise."

He grabbed her close.

"The newspaper brought this," he muttered, "some mistakes you never stop paying for." Carlie didn't know what mistakes her dad had made, but at that moment it became clear that the consequences would be hers to pay.

CHAPTER 2

Curly's Suit

The coin sang at the flick of Curly's thumb.

"Heads!" Mickey cried. He was ten years old and wore the typical combination of scuffed blue jeans and pocket T-shirt common to children in the 60s. In addition to his simple clothing, Mickey Haddon perpetually wore a sincere smile that brought out dimples on his cheeks. His eyes glistened with the honest mischief of all young boys, and though he didn't know it yet, his heart was good. He watched the coin tumble through the air and reflected on how deeply he enjoyed friendly activities with his jovial neighbor.

After flashing for a split second, the coin came down to land in Curly's palm with a satisfying smack. Curly completed the flip by slapping his hand down upon the back of his arm. He gave Mickey an anticipatory nod before lifting his hand away to reveal the result.

It was heads.

"By golly, that's ten in a row," Curly said with a laugh. He was a large man, not tall, but well-filled out. He had curly hair, of course, which he affected in the manner of a Caucasian Afro set off by a full beard. The result was that his head resembled a giant fuzzy tennis ball. Despite his saturnine and hirsute appearance, he was a gentle soul, respected by his peers at Kelley Construction. His friendship with Mickey had been cemented earlier that summer when they'd crowded around Curly's little TV to watch the moon landing. Curly treated Mickey more like a nephew than a neighbor. "Come on, kid, what's the trick?"

"There's no trick," Mickey replied. For the life of him, he couldn't understand why Curly kept asking him whether the coin would come up tails or heads. The game seemed pointless to Mickey since the answer was so obvious. Might as well ask the color of the grass or the sky.

"One more time," Curly said.

"Oh come on, Curly," Mickey replied, "let's play catch instead."

"Once more," Curly insisted with a smile, "heads or tails?"

"Neither."

Sensing victory, Curly sent the quarter spinning. As he reached to catch it, the quarter took an odd flip and bounced off Curly's finger to roll down the sidewalk and into the drain.

Curly sat stupefied for a moment before turning to look at Mickey with a respect that all of a sudden began to border on concern. For the first time, he seemed to realize this wasn't a trick.

"It might be better not to mention this to anyone," Curly said after a lengthy pause.

The big man's demeanor sent a chill down Mickey's spine. Curly had clearly been shaken on a profound level. Mickey didn't fully understand, but a child is sensitive to signs of an adult in distress, and he knew better than to push the issue. He resolved to keep his predictions to himself in the future.

***

A few weeks later, Mickey's resolve about suppressing his talent of foresight was put to its first test. Curiously, the incident revolved around his friendly neighbor's Brooks Brothers suit.

There was no need for a man of Curly's modest taste and lifestyle to own a good suit, so he didn't—until his wife put her foot down.

"Curly, with all due respect, I've spent thirty years going to weddings and reunions and holiday dances with a husband wearing jeans and a sweater. I'm getting you a suit for your birthday."

Curly's protests were in vain. A trip to Boston resulted in the purchase of a brown Brooks Brothers suit. Two hundred dollars changed hands; big money in those days. To everyone's surprise, Curly developed a sense of pride in his suit and looked forward to his few opportunities to wear it. But his social circle tended toward Friday night fish fries and trips to the bowling alley, so there was little call for his Brooks Brothers pride and joy. When not in use, the suit stayed well-pressed and safe in a plastic bag in the closet.

There are two types of people; those who preserve the few nice things they have, and those who view every one of their possessions as objects to be used and discarded. Curly's co-worker Wayne was a member of the second group.

Totally out of the blue, as was his wont, Wayne came over to Curly's house with a request.

"Curly, I like this woman. I want to make a good impression. Can I borrow your suit?"

Wayne resembled Curly, physically anyway. Emotionally, not so much. Whereas Curly exuded a quiet demeanor that put people at ease, Wayne was cold and distant. Wayne ignored children and seemed perpetually peeved. Nobody liked him, except Curly. Curly liked him in the way that kind-hearted souls adopt feral cats rather than let them suffer.

The request occurred in the driveway that Curly shared with Mickey Haddon. Mickey was there, playing in his yard, biding his time in the hope that Curly would have some time for catch later. Children did not exist as far as Wayne was concerned, so he didn't even notice the perceptive fourth grader.

Wayne's request to borrow the suit shocked Mickey as if he had touched the supernatural third rail. He experienced a physical sting as if his whole body was a funny bone and he'd just collided with a table. All the energy focused into a single point and burst out in an exclamation of surprising volume. "Don't let him!" Mickey howled.

The rebuke was so loud that Mickey's mom came running out of the house.

"What happened?" Mrs. Haddon said.

Curly and Wayne were regarding Mickey with very different expressions. Wayne's face reflected shock and confusion at the boy's outburst. Curly's face contained a resigned understanding. Curly was the first to speak.

"Ma'am, I think Mickey's a little upset about our conversation. It's our fault. We were talking about women."

Without giving Mickey a chance to explain, Mrs. Haddon grabbed her son by the ear. She pulled him into the kitchen, up the stairs, into his room and slammed the door. Mickey knew better than to protest. Instead, he grabbed a Big Chief tablet and a pencil and put down the first entry in a record of premonitions that would span many years.

Back outside, Mickey's outburst was just another in a long list of reasons Curly had to not lend out his suit. But he found his self-interest, as always, overruled by his gentle nature.

"Sure, Wayne, just have it dry-cleaned before you bring it back."

***

Mickey heard the final fate of Curly's suit a few days later while practicing his spy skills by eavesdropping on his parents after they thought he was asleep. From the top of the stairs, Mickey observed his dad sipping at his nightly shot of Old Crow while his mother enjoyed a modest few ounces of Gallo burgundy out of a purple Melmac coffee cup.

"You're not going to believe what happened today," Mr. Haddon said. "Curly stopped me in the driveway and told me about his latest misadventure with Wayne."

Mickey's mom took a drag off an unfiltered Chesterfield cigarette, her single one of the day. She was generally disinterested in news about Wayne, but she enjoyed a good piece of gossip as much as anyone. She settled back in a relaxed posture and exhaled a plume of smoke.

"Tell me about it."

"Apparently, Wayne had a terrible date and he decided to finish the evening by railroading Curly on the phone. The call came around 10 p.m., so you know what that means."

"Wayne had already had a few?"

Mickey's dad nodded. "More than a few if I know Wayne. Anyway, Wayne had borrowed Curly's suit for the date—"

"The Brooks Brothers suit?" Mrs. Haddon had an eye for fashionable things.

"Yup. Well, things weren't going well on the date and they got worse when Wayne yelled 'I wore my best suit for you!' at the poor woman."

"The nerve of that guy," Mickey's mom said, shaking her head.

"Well," the girl snapped, "'Clothes don't make the man!'"

"She's right about that..."

"And she stormed out."

"Good for her, but let me guess," Mrs. Haddon said. "Wayne is mad at Curly because the suit didn't work."

"Well, it's more complicated than that, get this. Curly hasn't been able to get the suit back."

"Oh no!"

"And he's not going to get it back."

"What do you mean?"

"Well, apparently Wayne got so worked up chewing Curly out on the phone he had a heart attack."

Mrs. Haddon was not without compassion. "Is he OK?"

"No, he's dead."

"Dead!"

"Yeah, he didn't come in to work, so the landlord went to investigate. Found him in bed." Mickey's dad knocked on the table as he took a drink. "Dead as a doornail. Kind of makes you think."

"I'm glad somebody found him at least," Mickey's mom said. "Guys like Wayne tend to go unmissed. But why didn't you start off by saying that Wayne died?"

"Well, this story isn't about Wayne; it's about Curly's suit. Wayne didn't have a nice suit and now he's in need of one again."

Mickey's mom went white. "Don't tell me..."

Her response was interrupted by a loud sneeze. It was Mickey, who had been trying to hold it in until the end of the story but couldn't quite get there. The conversation came to a halt as the young boy was escorted back to bed by the ear.

***

Wayne's visitation was on Friday.

The Haddons were a church-going family and so despite the fact that Mickey had never seen a dead body and did not want to start, his parents insisted they all go to pray for the deceased, and to support their friend Curly, whose kind nature had burdened him with an unwarranted sense of responsibility for Wayne's demise.

The Haddons showed up for the visitation early, intending to beat the rush. Their worries were unfounded because they were the first ones to walk up the steps to the door of the funeral home, a converted three-story house. Mickey followed his mom and dad up four gray wooden steps with the risers painted white, walked across the broad porch and entered. Mickey knew his parents had had a small argument over whether Wayne was deserving of fifty cents for a sympathy card. He knew the outcome when his mother went over to a small podium, signed the guest book and dropped a somber-looking Hallmark envelope into a slotted oaken box.

The entryway opened into a sitting room. There were a dozen folding chairs, all unoccupied except for one in which Wayne's mother sat. Wayne's sister stood by the casket. In the casket was Wayne. As they say, "He looked just like himself." He did look like himself. Himself in Curly's suit.

Mr. Haddon laughed.

Mrs. Haddon elbowed him. If Mickey's dad had been ten, she would have pulled his ear. It was clearly time to go. The family piled back into the car, mother and dad in the front and Mickey centered in the back seat. A somber mood didn't mean Mickey couldn't open his mouth and make it worse. The boy leaned over.

"Dad, this is weird. I'm worried."

"Nothing to worry about," Mr. Haddon answered. "A man died. It happens, ok?"

"No, no, Dad, not that. I mean I knew too much ahead of time…"

Mr. Haddon looked over his shoulder. "What in the hell are you talking about?"

The car came to a stop sign. Mickey reached over his dad's shoulder and put the Big Chief tablet in front of his face. He shook it.

"Dad! I knew something was going to happen. This is a problem."

"Get that thing out of my face, I'm trying to drive."

Mickey grew desperate and pointed insistently at the notebook. The words were dated the day of the driveway conversation. They said: "Curly is not going to get his suit back."

"Dad, look!" Mickey implored.

"Mickey, I can't see!" Mickey's dad howled. With a quick motion, he grabbed his son's tablet and threw it out the window. "Problem solved!"

They drove the rest of the way home in uncomfortable silence. Mickey did not get escorted to his room by the ear and for that he was grateful.

***

Later that afternoon, Mickey hopped onto his Schwinn Sting Ray, thumbed the Sturmey-Archer three speed shift lever into high gear and sped back to that corner. As he pedaled, the sting of his father's rejection slowly dissipated. He knew his dad to be a meat and potatoes guy, there was no room in his world view for extra-sensory perception.

Arriving at the corner, Mickey got lucky and found his tablet, half-buried in oak leaves in the gutter. A few pages had been blown out but not the important ones.

There was also something new. A sketch had appeared on one of the back pages. The sketch was of a little girl's face. She was holding her finger up to her lips and in a comic strip balloon coming out of her mouth was written, "Shhhhhh!"

Mickey didn't know what to make of the drawing, but Curly's warning and his dad's reaction had taught him a lesson about discussing things that didn't make sense. He kept making notes, but he resolved never to snow them to anyone. He kept that resolution for many years, never showing anyone until decades later during a fateful meeting at the Lenmel Hotel.

CHAPTER 3

Smoke

Mort LeFrance was conceived in the cab of a pickup truck in the parking lot of Folsom prison in the spring of 1946. His dad, Lenny, had been doing five for aggravated assault but secured an early release when he was offered the option of taking an experimental drug in exchange for an early parole. He never asked about the risk, and called the situation nothing more than "tossing back some shots for a bunch of skinny, limp-wrist, government pencil-pushers." Lenny was never much on details, so he neglected to ask the contents of the tincture he imbibed. Upon his release, as he stumbled through the Folsom gates he recalled seeing what years later in Haight-Ashbury would be called chem trails. He paid little attention, intent on expelling two years of pent-up frustration on his long-suffering wife, Sissy. Whatever drugs he'd been given came along for the ride and something was passed to his firstborn and only son, Mort.

Very early in his life, Mort began seeing things that weren't there. Generally the visions came to him in the form of smoke. He saw a haze invisible to others. The black mirage would twist and dance in the air like ink poured into water. Mort could watch the show for hours, and sometimes his mother would find him with a far-off look that seemed to focus on everything and nothing all at once.

The toughening of Mort began early. The more he was beaten, the angrier he became. He was a hellion with everyone except his mother. To the rest, he was a malevolent force of nature, just like his dad. That worked fine on the playground because he was bigger and tougher than all the other kids. No one ever made fun of his club foot more than once.

He grew tall and lanky with shoulder-length hair and knuckles perpetually scuffed from work or fights.

Mort was in his late teens when he rolled in to watch the 49ers game at the 81-Z where his mother worked. He should have been in school, but he'd been kicked out. He was too young to drink but that had never stopped him before.

"What'll ya have?" asked Sissy with a tender smile.

"Anchor Steam," Mort replied.

Sissy winked and lifted the selection from behind the bar. She'd had it ready.

Mort kept one eye on the smeary screen and the other on Sissy as she strolled away to the other customers. There was a drunk sailor down at the end who was watching Sissy with more intensity than Mort cared to allow.

The screen above crackled as the announcers began to spout their endless verbal refuse.

"They should play these games without narration," Mort mumbled. "All I want to hear is the sound of helmets crashing and cries of impact. I can't take the false poetry of these TV punks."

Nobody answered. That meant nothing to Mort; he was used to talking to himself.

He glanced to the end of the bar just in time to see the sailor slap Sissy on the behind. Sissy jumped as if stung and the sailor flashed her a lecherous smile. Mort made sure to look away before Sissy glanced in his direction. He wanted to allow her the dignity of pretending it had never happened, but he clenched his jaw so tight his teeth hurt. He took a flavorless swig of his Anchor Steam and tried hard to keep his hand from trembling.

Over the course of years, Mort had lost all tolerance for any sort of physical aggression against his mother. Mort's old man, Lenny, was never slow to raise his hand against either mother or child. Mort's early attempts to defend Sissy were successful only in drawing attention onto himself. After those beatings, Lenny would usually take off to this very bar. In those moments, Sissy would hold Mort close and try to quench the fire inside him.

Rinse, dry, repeat.

Comfort was harder to come by when Mort reached puberty and became too big to cuddle. Sometimes Mort feared his rage was so insatiable that he might take it out on his mother, so he took to leaving the house.

"And here's the kickoff!" the announcer blathered.

Mort glanced up to watch the ball go high, high, high into the air and then plummet down into the hands of the returner, who took two steps before nearly getting his head taken off by a gunner who hit him at full speed.

The returner lay still on the grass as his teammates waved for the trainers.

A few minutes later, the returner was hauled off on a stretcher and the game resumed. Mort liked the kickoff the best.

"Need a refill?" Sissy asked.

"Not yet, thanks, Mom."

Growing up, Mort had not had much supervision. When he ran into problems with authority at school, which became more frequent as he aged, he would take days off and find trouble around town. He'd wander along the docks where hundreds of houseboats were moored. Eventually the sewage and noise and chaos of the floating neighborhood caused a crackdown. The houseboats got cleaned up, and the fleet became a fraction of what used to be docked in Sausalito. In Mort's childhood, the docks area was a city unto itself, populated by free spirits, beatniks, musicians, artists, retirees, and grifters. Interesting types who did not want to be tied down to dry land. Mort learned a lot of lessons there; some of them hard.

Mort never finished high school. He was combustible. As a freshman, the high school staff held him in check by suspending him whenever he went off the rails and beat up other kids, but when he punched out a teacher his sophomore year, he was expelled. At his final expulsion hearing, his principal said to his parents in front of Mort, "Mark my words. This young man is ruthless." Sissy cried. Lenny spit on the floor and said, "He's too good for this soft school. You can't kick him out. We quit."

Back up on the big screen, the 49ers lasted three plays and had to punt. At the end of the bar, the sailor cried out in disgust, "What a bunch of losers!" He then pushed himself away from the bar and stumbled into the bathroom.

Mort tipped his beer back again; the bottle trembled less now. Without realizing it, Mort issued a low whistle as he put the empty bottle back on the bar: a long single note that he bent slightly higher at the end.

Back in school, he'd gotten into the habit of whistling. He could do it like a songbird. As the years passed his whistling became sinister, so much so that it preceded him like the ticking clock of the crocodile in Peter Pan.

He began running away. His parents were not around, so it was easy to skip out. Lenny would be out riding with the boys and Mom would be working one of her two jobs, trying to keep food on the table. When the boy did not show up, Lenny would go find him and another beating would ensue, until one night when Mort was fourteen and six-foot-two, he hit the old man in the head with the chain he used to lock his bike—knocking him out. Lenny was drunk and between the concussive whack of the chain and the beer, he hit the deck and stayed there until morning. When he woke up, he went up to Mort's room, looked in and said, "You're old enough to start riding with us. I'll have a hog for you tonight. Get ready."

That night, the club pickup truck pulled up in front of Lenny's house and the boys rolled out a stolen softail; a classic motorcycle of the day. They showed Mort how to kick-start it and had him follow them down to Big Sur, where they stopped and told him to go in and rob the liquor store. No problem. He walked in with the bicycle chain and walked out with eighty-seven dollars cash and two bottles of Jack Daniels.

Mort had lost interest in the 49ers' game. He pushed himself away from the bar and headed in the direction of the bathroom.

Riding with the Angels brought a sense of purpose for a while, but it didn't last. Around the fringes, Mort always had a vision of the smoke. With time, the dancing ink became clearer, more sinister, and impossible to escape. He could see faces, he could see acts.

Mort came to understand that Lenny was pure evil. Sissy was not. Mort suffered an unbearable tension caused by enjoying his father's gift of bullying and hurting on the one hand, and nursing a love for his mother that went so deep that when he thought about it, emotion welled up inside him as if he were going to throw up. He took his inner conflict on long strolls down by the dock and tried to let it out in low, haunting whistles.

Most men were bad. The smoke showed him that. Striking first became self-defense when you had premonitions of what was to come. They all had it coming, and would respond tenfold if given the chance.

The bathroom door creaked open as Mort entered. It was a smallish room with cheap fixtures.

"Hey, buddy," the sailor said, "I think there's only room for one."

Mort glanced around and nodded. He stepped forward and shut the door.

"I'll be done in a minute," the sailor said, glancing back without turning his head.

When the sailor resumed focus on his business, Mort hit him with the chain. He hit the sailor much harder than he had hit his dad or the liquor store owner. The sailor lurched forward over the urinal before slumping back down onto the tiles, still clutching his manhood in his hand.

The sailor wouldn't be getting up anytime soon.

Mort was smart enough to keep on going out the backdoor and not even Sissy ever really knew what had happened. Walking home, Mort wondered if he had killed the man. He felt a tingling anticipation. The darkness at the fringes of his consciousness came tighter into focus and soothed him.

"You've done right," it seemed to say. "He shouldn't have treated Sissy that way. He got what he had coming."

It was the smoke talking, but the words came out in Mort's voice, low and quiet like a sad whistle.

CHAPTER 4

Carlie

If Carlie had received the same advice Mickey got from Curly, perhaps there would have been less pain in her life. But instead of a pragmatic neighbor to rely on for guidance, she had Alan and Shalla Stillman, loving parents who sometimes let curiosity get the better of them.

Alan had met Shalla when they were undergrads at Stanford. They were both after their doctorate; Alan in biochemistry and Shalla in psychology. Like many men in those days, Alan's career had started in the military, but the end of World War II had kept him from seeing any combat. His involvement with the military continued in some capacity that Shalla didn't understand. Whenever she queried Alan on the matter, he dodged the questions. It became clear to Shalla that some part of Alan's work required confidentiality, which she came to accept as a condition of knowing him. Shalla was busy enough with the demands of her own career, and as long as the bills were paid, she decided she didn't need to know.

As a hobby, Alan had an interest in parapsychology which, when brought up in social gatherings of academic colleagues, always elicited a round of nervous coughs and hastily contrived excuses to withdraw. Alan's work kept him busy. Sometimes the phone would ring in the middle of the night and Shalla would hear Alan's indecipherable muttering in the study, only to have him return to bed tight-lipped and pallid.

They were married January 1st, 1950 because that made it easy for Alan to remember their anniversary. Typical of academic couples, they had children late; Robert was born in '55 with Carlie coming along in '58.

Carlie's first childhood memory was of the phone ringing, except it had not rung.

"Grandma's on the phone," she told her mother, despite being an infant new to words. There was the kind of excitement in her voice that made Shalla pay attention, although she thought the girl was playing make-believe.

"Oh," Shalla said, "what does she have to say?"

"Ask her yourself," Carlie replied.

Then the phone rang and Shalla picked it up. "Oh, hi Mom, we were just talking about you." Shalla paused and gave Carlie a puzzled look, but Carlie had already returned to her innocent playing.

The second time Carlie predicted a phone call, Shalla took it more seriously. On the third occasion, Shalla mentioned the phenomenon to Alan.

"Hmmm," Alan said, neither accepting nor dismissing the story. He merely pulled out a graph paper notebook and began making entries.

When a supposition becomes data, it's easy for a conclusion to change. Still, there were factors to be considered. Having been a mother herself, Shalla's mom knew not to call during nap time. Also, Carlie didn't make predictions for other callers. It could have been a simple coincidence that Carlie called out for her grandma just before the phone rang. More careful observation would reveal what was happening.

After a year of record keeping, Alan discovered some trends. If Carlie's declarations were random, it followed there would be occasions when she predicted a call that never came.

But Carlie was never wrong, nor did she fail to anticipate Grandma's call.

"There's something different about our child," Alan told Shalla. "She has a gift, and it's our job to help her develop it."

Shalla and Alan were both well-versed in doing research. Their small home was stacked with books, magazines and inter-library loan articles. As caring parents, they did their best to guide their exceptional daughter through a world they themselves could not see.

With encouragement, Carlie's gift began to develop.

The incident with the golf ball took things to a different level.

Carlie was in the backyard playing with her older brother Robert. She worshiped Robert, even though he could be a careless jerk. Bob was forbidden from driving golf balls in the backyard, but he wheedled his dad into allowing him to hit little chip shots.

Alan had noticed Bob's swings getting more aggressive over time, but he ignored it because Bob was a skinny, uncoordinated kid and Alan thought the activity would do him good. Anyway, most of the time Bob's swings failed to connect with the ball solidly enough to impart any meaningful force, but even a blind pig finds a truffle once in a while.

On that afternoon, the boy gave a Herculean swing and nailed the Titleist with the edge of his nine iron with the kind of perfect inaccuracy that results in a 10 yard chip shot becoming an 80 yard line drive. The impact of the club against the ball elicited a disharmonic click, and the ball took off like a space experiment.

Carlie was about twenty feet away, standing on tiptoes, trying to reach an apple on the tree near the fence line. Just as Bob swung, Carlie squatted for no apparent reason. The ball rifled through the empty space where her head had been.

The note struck by the golf club got Alan's attention and he'd started running toward Carlie with the extra speed granted when parental adrenaline starts pumping through the veins. He saw Carlie duck, and arrived half a heartbeat later to embrace her in a grateful hug.

"Are you OK, honey?"

"Yes, Dad, I'm fine," Carlie said, somewhat annoyed at the interruption in her attempt to pluck the apple from the bough above her.

"You almost got brained by a golf ball!" Alan was still hardly able to believe disaster had been averted. "Why did you duck like that?"

Carlie shrugged. "I felt a need to duck."

Alan shook his head, and as the sweet flutter of adrenaline began to ebb from his bloodstream, he turned his attention to Bob. Bob was standing frozen in the follow-through of his swing, looking at his father and sister with glossy eyes. Alan's own eyes narrowed, and Bob, not needing to be told, realized driving practice had been canceled until further notice.

That evening, Alan turned to Shalla. "Are you familiar with what Jung called synchronicity?"

Shalla put down the magazine she had been paging through and fixed Alan with a stern look full of skepticism. "Meaningful coincidences that give us a glimpse of universal connectivity?"

"I've always been somewhat doubtful of the idea myself," Alan said.

"You should be, it's pseudo-science. It's the kind of nonsense you spout at a convention to generate publicity when you have a book coming out. I thought you were done with that kind of thing."

Alan's face showed a hint of anger, and Shalla backtracked to more stable ground.

"At the end of the day," she said, "an untestable idea cannot be the foundation to a scientific theory no matter how eloquently or sincerely it's restated."

"I didn't bring it up as an example of truth, but more as a model for a starting point."

Shalla gave Alan a dark look. "If this is your way of grooming me to the idea of bringing our little girl into the world of psycho-babble, you can forget it."

"No, I don't mean that." Alan switched tactics for a smoother approach. "There might be something going on with Carlie that can affect her life and happiness. What if she needs assistance? Assistance that we are not equipped to provide for her?"

Shalla softened. Alan had touched on the essential parental dilemma. But she wasn't without her counter-arguments. "Could it be that the abilities you see in her are just a projection of your own fixation on parapsychology?"

"You're the one who noticed her predictions, not me."

Shalla's face hardened. "I won't allow you to take her into the lab and put electrodes on her skull so your colleagues can stare at her brain waves while they wait for the phone to ring."

"Absolutely not," Alan said. "I'm not trying to do this in secret, Shalla; I'm discussing this with you. Nothing happens without your approval and involvement."

"You're right it doesn't!" Shalla snapped.

"But what about the other side of the argument? Do we want to impede her development? Should we make her suppress her abilities? What effect might that have?"

"I'm not sure the world is ready for an individual who can predict the future. She might be labeled a freak, ostracized from her community..."

"So you're saying we should teach her to be something she's not?" Alan said. "Teach her to hide what she truly is? That's worked out so well throughout history. Maybe we should do some reading about individuals with non-traditional sexual orientation living within fundamental, conservative societies. What psychoses develop when people are bludgeoned into hiding their true nature?"

"That's not the same," Shalla said.

"It's exactly the same! We can't just consider Carlie; we have to consider how people will perceive her. You know as well as I do that the social contract is just a thread suspending us over a pit of barbarism. It takes very little to cut the safeguards, and once the fall begins, the acceleration is terrible. Nothing terrifies people more than something they cannot understand."

"This is just an argument you're using to make me agree with you."

"Don't deflect," Alan replied. "I didn't give Carlie her gifts, but she has them and we need to address it. I'm asking for your help and your input."

Shalla took a deep breath. "What do you propose?"

"I think we need to engage in private study. We continue keeping the records we've started, but widen the net. How many times has Carlie shown flashes of ability that we haven't even noticed? We have to explore what she's capable of and evaluate it without our parental emotion clouding the picture. The data will ground us. First of all we have to figure out what she can do. Can she guide her predictions or are they involuntary? Is she capable of reading minds? What about telekinesis? Most of all, can she develop her gift? Does she control it? How can we help her?"

Shalla nodded slowly. She still had a mother's misgivings, but even the most skeptical part of her nature understood that ignoring Carlie's gift could only be labeled an act of cowardice. In the end she agreed, and the observations began.

Carlie was nine at the time and her flashes of precognition were getting stronger by the day. She never told them, but she recognized a change in her parents when they began taking notes. A few years later while walking home down an oak-lined street from a friend's house, she found a Big Chief tablet in the gutter. Without knowing why, she flipped over a page and sketched a face and bubbled in a cartoon lettered, "Shhhhhh!" She sensed she was reaching out to an unknown friend, and in a way she couldn't explain, she felt her concerns about her parents' change of attitude seep into the drawing. She didn't tell her parents about the notebook or what she felt. As a result, the incident never made its way into her daddy's graph paper recordings.

By the time Carlie had entered eighth grade, Alan had enough data to crunch the numbers and look for correlations. He ran analyses of variation studies and statistically concluded that there was less than .005 percent chance that all of the coincidental moments involving Carlie were random.

At that point, Alan's scholarly excitement got the better of him. He took diligent notes as he worked with the numbers, and every time he revised them the syntax became cleaner and the conclusions became more obvious. The notes became something of an obsession over the next few months as he passed over them again and again. One day he took a step back from his work and was surprised to discover that the notes had the potential to become a compelling and well-researched academic article. He completed the work without really understanding why.

He scrawled an address upon an envelope and inserted the article with the rationalization that the input of a larger community could be nothing but beneficial.

Grabbing his jacket from the hook at his entryway, Alan made the short walk to the post office. Placing the letter upon the lip of the blue container, he paused.

He hadn't consulted Shalla on this development. Should he have?

It was just a short note being sent to an obscure journal that nobody read. Anyway, the article was far more likely to wind up in a trash can than see the light of day within the pages of the publication.

He let the letter fall. The white rectangle drifted down into the blackness and out of Alan's control forever.

***

Months later, Carlie's mother answered the phone.

A woman's voice said, "Hello, is this Shalla Stillman?"

"Yes."

There was a brief pause. "Please don't hang up, this is Ruth Nooker and I really have to tell you something."

Shalla hesitated. She recognized the name; Ruth was a journalism student Shalla had taken a restraining order out against a few years ago when she was working with Alan on one of his projects for the

Stanford labs. Every instinct compelled Shalla to slam down the phone. Whether her hesitation was from the plea in Ruth's voice or a sense of personal culpability, Shalla couldn't be sure.

Ruth, a competent journalist, took advantage of the pause.

"I'm sorry to have made you uncomfortable in the past, but I have new information about that night in L.A."

Shalla didn't encourage the woman by responding.

"I was dancing with the woman in the accident…" Ruth's voice trailed off.

Shalla winced.

She remembered.

A woman had wandered off from an LSD control group and been run over and killed.

"I can't comment on that, the subjects were promised anonymity," Shalla said, finding her voice.

"I'm not asking you to comment," Ruth said, "there's something you need to know."

Again, Shalla didn't reply.

Ruth continued. "The woman was there with her son, we were all dancing together. He was a tall, raw-boned young biker…"

Shalla heard Ruth take a deep breath to collect herself.

"There was something about him… He moved with a muscular intensity that would have been almost…" Ruth paused to search for a word, "beautiful if he wasn't always a half step off beat. He had a club foot that would not behave…"

Shalla found herself wiping a tear from her eye. She hadn't expected to be forced to confront the mistakes of her past that morning, and long ago she had stopped any effort to push Alan for answers. She took a deep breath. "I'm sorry, but I don't think I have anything further to add."

"Wait, wait," Ruth replied. "I never got a chance to tell you that I thought he was dangerous. I can't tell you why, just a feeling. You need to take him seriously, especially with the article that's about to come out in *The Daily Register.*"

A spike of anger restored Shalla's backbone. "What article?"

"Your husband published a journal article about your daughter Carlie and her special abilities."

"He did what?" Shalla snapped.

"You didn't know?"

Shalla's jaw clenched and even through the silence transmitted through the phone, Ruth could sense her rage. Shalla wrestled with her emotions for a lengthy interval before finally managing a response. "You keep my daughter out of the paper," Shalla replied.

"It was an assignment, it was an assignment!" Ruth replied, half yelling. "The general public always has an appetite for parapsychology, especially when a local person manifests such talents. Your husband should have expected some interest when he published. It was just in a small, scholarly journal. My article will bring your husband's paper to larger prominence."

"You have no right. . ."

"Don't be foolish, your husband put the name in the public record, not me. I'm calling as a courtesy," Ruth replied. "Nothing publicly stated by you or anyone else suggests my article will put anyone in any danger."

Shalla inhaled hard enough for Ruth to hear over the receiver.

"Then why are you calling?"

"Would you like to go on record now?" Ruth's tone was deadly serious. "Is there something you know that you've kept secret? Is there something to be scared of?"

Shalla paused. Years of living with her husband flashed through her thoughts. Late arrivals, midnight phone calls, and his sharp retorts when she tried to engage him in conversation. They'd been married many years, and the coping mechanisms were not so easily brushed aside. Not even for the sake of her daughter.

"Never call me again," she said, before placing the phone on the cradle with a shaking hand. For a long while she sat staring at it helplessly.

CHAPTER 5

The Pranksters

Mort often saw the darkness when he was riding. It stretched out before him, beckoning into the distance. He'd long since given up efforts to avoid it. The shifty black smoke had a way of putting itself in his path. One evening, out front of their run-down trailer, his old man, Lenny, started longing for the road.

"Sissy, Mort, let's ride," Lenny bellowed, kick-starting his hog and gesturing at the highway.

"What's the rush?" Mort replied. With numb curiosity, he thought he perceived a smoky thread trailing off in the direction Lenny's bike pointed. He shook his head to clear it as he swung his leg over his own ride.

"Our brothers have made friends with some fancy college types, call themselves the Pranksters. They've got a free party going on in L.A., all expenses paid. I figured we should make an appearance just in case they start thinking they're tough."

"Those college types ain't your friends, Len," Mort said. "They ain't got enough vertebrae to make a spine between them, but they're devious. They don't see folks like us as quite human, you know. We're more like rodents to them, lesser beasts to be used and discarded."

"Yeah, well, we'll smoke their dope and drink their beer and kick their ass if they start showing attitude. Like I said, it's a free party."

Mort shrugged. Sissy climbed on behind Lenny.

Mort almost forgot his preoccupations as they hauled along down Highway 101. Sissy switched back and forth between Len and Mort, and Mort appreciated having his mom sit behind him and share the road. He could feel her heartbeat as she leaned against him, and that provided the kind of comfort nothing else could.

Arriving at the venue, they parked their rides and followed the "acid test" signs until they got to the school gymnasium. Inside, a band was playing, loud. People danced and Len cracked a smile. "Shoot, they look wasted already," he said, and wandered off into the crowd to impose some shuffling dance moves on unsuspecting coeds.

A middle-aged man in a Stanford sweater approached Mort and Sissy. Something about him caused alarm bells to go off in Mort's mind, and his eyes narrowed.

"Welcome," the man said.

Mort nodded.

The man in the Stanford sweater lifted his hands and made a couple awkward dance steps before sauntering off into the crowd.

"Honey," Sissy said, "this noise is getting to me, I need some water."

Concerned by his mom's distress, Mort grabbed the nearest hippie by his shirt and blue jean vest and pulled him close.

"Hey, man, where can I get some water or something?"

The hippie tugged back against Mort's grasp with unnecessary force and Mort could feel the fabric give.

"Look out, you Neanderthal!" the hippie cried. "Look what you did to my shirt!"

Mort's body tensed in a way that made the hippie recoil. Mort took half a step forward and the man with the torn shirt flinched. Before the lean biker could continue his advance, a woman's hand met his chest.

Mort turned to the person belonging to the hand and his gaze came to rest on an attractive woman also in a Stanford sweater.

"Hi, I'm Shalla. Can I help?"

"You're one of the scientists, aren't you?" Mort asked.

Shalla shrugged.

Mort had already had enough of the cutesy attitude. "Mom doesn't feel well. She needs something to take an aspirin with."

Shalla looked at the suffering woman. "I can get her some water."

"Just show me where it is," Mort replied.

Shalla nodded and pointed past the table in the center of the gym with the coolers of LSD-laced Kool-Aid to a water bubbler on the far gym wall.

"Let me lead you," Shalla said, reaching for Sissy's arm. Mort slapped her hand away.

"I can handle this."

Mort stalked off with his mother.

Shalla watched them go, expecting them to circumvent the LSD coolers and proceed to the bubbler beyond. To her horrified surprise, Mort instead stopped at the table and handed his mom a Dixie cup of the Kool-Aid drink.

"Stop!" Shalla screamed, but her voice was washed out in the overwhelming blast of music and partying that swept across the room. She pushed her way through the throng to assist the young man and his mother, but found every dancing shoulder aligned to oppose her.

Mort was pleased that the cool drink seemed to calm his mom. A guy behind the counter offered him a Dixie cup as well, but he pushed it aside, knowing such a trifle would never quench his appetites. He lifted a pitcher by the handle and tilted back his head for a long swallow.

"What are you doing, man? That can kill you!" a Prankster said, reaching to stop the biker from drinking.

Mort shoved the Prankster back over the table. The table collapsed, drinks spilling everywhere. A couple of brawnier Pranksters made an attempt at subduing Mort, and he tossed them as well. The harder the shoves came, the further they ranged, and more and more people got involved in the brawl.

Shalla tried to shove through the crowd, but she couldn't make any progress. The noise was immense, the room was huge, and the small explosion of violence continued to gain momentum unchecked. In the heat of battle, Mort lost track of his mom.

***

In the midst of the chaos surrounding Mort, there was a cloud of calm emanating from Sissy. She lifted her hand to her forehead and began drifting through the blobs of color that weaved and danced around her.

Sissy felt like she was floating. The floor dropped below her and then slid sideways, and it was all she could do to keep her balance. She stumbled over to the corner of the gym and found a dark spot where she sat down in a futile attempt to get herself together.

Minutes passed that seemed like seasons. Sissy had a vague recollection that she had been accompanied, but now that memory seemed like a dream.. She stood again and headed outside, where she spotted a bicycle lying on the ground. She lifted the object from the ground amidst childhood recollections of riding with a pack of friends down to the lake to while away a summer's day in careless play. Although she could barely walk, she flung her leg over the top tube, surprised to find that she could balance on the bicycle perfectly. She began to pedal. A slight breeze cooled her face and she felt an overwhelming sense of peace.

Sissy smiled.

She looked down. The tires of her bicycle appeared to be three feet off the ground. She was flying!

***

The noise of the party had brought the police, and several of them stood, ready in their riot gear, for when things inevitably took a turn for the worse. One police officer took his gaze off of the auditorium that seemed to be reverberating like a giant sub-woofer. He gave the surroundings a quick scan, and paused when he noticed a a small woman wobbling back and forth on an old bicycle. The woman was accelerating into a crosswalk. Acting on instinct, the cop began to run, the desperate run of a man who knows he's going to arrive too late.

"Lady!" he cried, gasping for breath. "Lady, stop! There's a bus!"

But Sissy didn't stop and she didn't see the bus. It hit her full on as she coasted through the crosswalk with a crash of broken bones and shattered glass that was quickly swallowed up by the throbbing music. By the time the cop arrived, there was nothing to do but scream for something to cover up what was left.

***

Back in the gym, Mort's dose had hit high gear. The black cloud coalesced around him. His blast furnace metabolism melted the raw ore of the psychedelic drug and transformed it into a molten fury. The smoke which had forever plagued his vision now seemed to be magnified by the concoction in the drink. The lazy suggestions of his premonitions, calcified into desperate orders impossible to ignore. Mort saw carbon bubbles above everyone's heads with words spelling out their thoughts and deeds. He quivered for a moment as he observed. Much of what he saw was evil. Clean-cut young men stood before him with sanguine smiles on their faces, but within the dark clouds Mort watched them transform into cackling demons with daggers for teeth and hollow shadows instead of eyes.

Mort took raging gasps of air, caught somewhere between terror and rage. He glanced this way and that in awe of his newfound power.

Then, at once, all the bubbles shattered into ash and went floating like black snow to the ground. There was the echo of thunder exploding in his brain. Something had happened, a cosmic rip that split Mort in two. The smoke gave name to his greatest fear.

"Sissy! Mom's been hurt!"

The smoke urged him on and Mort charged toward the door, pushing bodies out of his way like a raging animal. They moved, but not fast enough, so Mort pulled his Bowie and began to slash left and right. Images of ghouls hovered over every face that caught his blade, and Mort knew he was doing right. But even with the sting of his knife and the spatter of blood, the raging throng did not part to his satisfaction. Mort alternated between his swinging fist and his slashing knife, cutting a path to the door and his mother in need of help.

"Move!" he bellowed.

His insanity forged a path, and the biker sprinted toward the nearest exit sign. He heard bells, a tinkling, and felt ice crystals cooling his fevered brow. Others saw wicked shards of glass embed themselves in his face and arms. Mort had crashed through a glass door without knowing.

Emergency vehicles had already arrived. The sirens wailed and bars of light flashed through Mort's throbbing skull. He couldn't decipher what was before him, and that added terror to his already long list of uncontrolled emotions.

In a tinted window, Mort caught a glimpse of a raging animal, arms reaching out, blood streaming from shards of glass embedded in his face. The slivers were so large that they twinkled red and blue with the light of the rescue vehicles. With a start, Mort realized he was looking at his own reflection.

"Look out!" a paramedic yelled, and then Mort crashed through a zebra-striped sawhorse barricade and fell upon a group of responders working on a body. Even in the chaos of light and sound Mort recognized his mother's form and ran to her. A cop grabbed his arm.

In his heightened awareness, Mort could see his mother's soul drifting away. The impediment on his arm enraged him. He turned on the cop, seeking to extricate himself as quickly and violently as possible. The patrolman flew through the air, and Mort continued on his charge.

Seeing what had happened, other officers dove forward to tackle Mort. He strode on, determined to get to his mother as body after body attached itself to him. He felt the blows of billy clubs raining down; he heard the dim thuds of wood, rubber, plastic and metal against his numb flesh.

Mort roared like an avenging angel. The men opposing him redoubled their efforts in terror. Still Mort advanced, and would have been impossible to stop, but it was '65 and the L.A. Police were well trained in applying a chokehold. A club was thrust under Mort's chin and a massive forearm clutched against his ear, drawing the wood against his windpipe.

Mort fell to his knees, then flat on his face, breaking his nose. His mom's broken body lay in a mangled mass before him. Grasping desperately at consciousness, Mort saw, beyond his mother, Lenny now charging as if in slow motion toward the fray.

By then the cops had had enough. Lenny stabbed the first, and at the howl of pain and splash of blood, weapons which had been drawn to be used on Mort were now turned on Lenny. Three shots hit the raging angel, two in the torso. Lenny went down.

***

The aftermath came into focus over the course of several days.

Mort spent two chained in a cell. Insane thrashing and howls reverberating against porcelain tiles purged the LSD from his ravaged system. Every now and then nurses arrived to pump him full of Thorazine, but the acid had awakened something in Mort that he somehow knew would never again fall into hibernation.

When the fog cleared, Mort was surprised to learn his father had survived, minus a kidney and his spleen. Mort expected to go to jail, but apparently some powerful people with influence didn't want an inquiry into the acid-test bloodbath. Mort sensed government involvement, only they were above the consequence of wrongful action, but he didn't complain when he was cut loose. The same would have been true of Lenny if he hadn't already had a record and several outstanding warrants. There were limits even to what the government could cover up. Lenny went to San Quentin.

His father's face haunted him. Mort could see it when he closed his eyes. That cold, unyielding stare, and his merciless voice croaking, "Watch out for your mom!"

His father would kill him!

But Lenny was in prison, and even he wasn't enough of a devil to deal a killing strike through a concrete wall.

Three months after Sissy's death, Mort went to visit his father. Lenny was brought to a security booth. The glass was so thick that phones had to be used for communication.

Mort sat down. He was still having LSD flashbacks and, at first, he wasn't completely sure if the conversation was happening in real life or on television.

"I can explain," Mort said.

Lenny's scowl gave way to a look of puzzlement.

Didn't he know about Sissy?

At the pause, Len's face hardened. Any thought Mort had of hiding the truth flew from him. He *knew!* Now he knew. He only needed it confirmed.

"What happened to your mother?" Len asked.

"She's dead."

Lenny's hands tightened on the phone until his knuckles went white. He sat there, trembling for a few moments, gaining steam. Then he howled. Mort could hear the howl even through the bulletproof glass. Len sprang at the glass, phone in hand, beating it against the surface with a superhuman rage as tears streamed down his face and the walls echoed with his cries.

Guards swarmed in, on both sides of the glass. The ones surrounding Mort simply put their hands on his shoulder. Through the glass, they pounced on Lenny, wrestling him into a chokehold and pulling him, kicking, away from the room. But still Len screamed with such a tortured voice that Mort could hear.

"You killed your mother, Mort, it was you!"

CHAPTER 6

The Tutor

The very rigid Catholic beliefs of Mickey's mother, along with her fear of the "wildness" of public schools, ensured Mickey would endure a long tenure at St. Asors Catholic grade school. St. Asors was an old three-story brick building located a short bike ride away from Mickey's home. It was the kind of antiquated construction that featured tall windows that opened by crank and chain rather than levers. Whenever a nun called for a window to be opened, Mickey would jump at the chance. He loved cranking on the mechanism and watching the chain wobble and sway as it served its purpose. There was plenty of opportunity for imagination at St. Asors. Although the lawns were always well-tended, the building sat like an ominous, indomitable fortress. Mickey felt slightly intimidated as he approached in the morning. He wondered what was contained in the attic rooms; secret places betrayed only by small, dark, outside windows. Were there cells up there? Libraries filled with books of magic? Torture chambers? He never quite worked up the courage to escape his daily schedule and explore.

The building leered at him in judgment, and over the years the fact that Mickey was repeatedly allowed to enter without being struck by lightning gave him a certain kind of confidence that he must be not that bad after all.

Students of St. Asors categorized themselves into two groups: the "tourists" and the "founders." Tourists were students who had spent some time in public schools. Usually these came in for a semester or a year before moving on to parts unknown. If the nuns were to be believed, their souls would fall straight into the clutches of torment and temptation the moment they slipped away from the hallowed halls of St. Asors. The nuns never went so far as to say the students were doomed, but they'd affect very troubled looks and wring their hands a lot if you pressed them for details. It might have been an act, but it was convincing.

Mickey was a founder. He'd been at St. Asors since his first day of school and would be one of the few to complete the program in its entirety.

Mickey didn't know whether to pity or envy the tourists. The woeful pantomime of the nuns could not erase the fact that tourist students always seemed to look forward to their escape. The students who had been in public schools always had a glint of mischief in their eyes. Mickey suspected they'd seen behind the curtain. The nuns often called the tourists "troublemakers." Mickey didn't know who was bluffing and who was telling the truth, so he toed the line.

In some ways, Catholic school was a much better fit for Mickey than public school could ever have been. He kept making his scribbles in his Big Chief notebook about strange occurrences, and might have thought himself crazy if he wasn't exposed to stories of the exceptional on a daily basis. Catholic school has a hyper focus on mysteries and the supernatural. Every day Mickey heard about people walking through rocks, rising from the dead, turning water into wine, curing leprosy with a touch, etc. It was almost enough to make Mickey doubt Curly's advice about maintaining silence. But he hadn't forgotten his dad's reaction, so Mickey was content to bide his time. Writing in his notebook also seemed to calm his desires to seek a confidant. Still, stories of the ancient world made him inclined to revere his own experiences rather than fear them. He developed a sense that these mysteries were among the types of things that just happened sometimes.

One afternoon, on his way to class, Mickey caught a snippet of a whispered conversation between Sister Angelica and Sister Isabel about a strange occurrence.

"The phone rang," Angelica said, "and I just knew who it was and what they were going to say."

Isabel didn't deny the statement or look skeptical; she just stood and offered a comforting hand upon Angelica's shoulder.

"Sure enough, it was Doctor Michael. Grandma had been failing for a long time, but still..."

Mickey walked out of earshot, unwilling to risk punishment to slow and hear more, but he'd gotten the gist. He'd shared the experience

Sister Angelica described, and it heartened him to hear an authority figure admit such a thing was real.

Six years endured under the fierce tutelage of Dominican nuns had a profound effect on Mickey. The nuns seemed huge in their black and white habits with rosaries hanging all the way to the floor. The kids were stuffed into classrooms of fifty, sixty, and sometimes seventy students. Like animals, they had to be made afraid of their masters.

The main instrument of law enforcement was the old triangular ruler. A good crack across the knuckles would get most students in line. For the naughtiest there was always the full swat across the back of the head.

Every morning, Mickey stood by his desk, recited the pledge of allegiance, an Our Father and a Hail Mary, and then sat down on command. His desk was old enough to have an inkwell on the top. The inkwell was empty because the nuns did not trust the children with open containers of any kind. However, the children were allowed cartridge fountain pens, which were perfect for spraying ink across the aisle and onto a neighbor's starched white shirt.

They obeyed a militant agenda without question until one morning, after the Hail Mary, the command to sit did not come. Instead, Sister Angelica cleared her throat. "Class, I would like you to welcome Sister Ann Winifred's eighth grade students. They will be coming to tutor you."

With that, the door opened and in walked an orderly file of kids who were only two grades ahead but who might as well have been grown-ups as far as Mickey was concerned. The boys at the front had the kind of disheveled hair and haughty smirk that made Mickey instinctively dread this whole tutoring idea. The entire enterprise seemed conceived to cultivate failure for the purpose of justifying sadistic torture. Mickey had almost completely committed to the path of total resistance when his gaze traveled to the back of the line and came to rest upon a cute brunette girl wearing a ponytail tied up in a light blue ribbon.

She might as well have been married and living in a foreign land, she appeared so unattainable. But just the sight of her, standing there real and delicate, changed the aspect of Mickey's whole reality. One by one the nuns assigned tutors to students. They grabbed arms and swung bodies over to their younger charges with the same strength and diligence that might be applied in disposing of bags of yard clippings.

Boy was assigned to boy, girl to girl, again and again until there remained only one boy, Mickey, and only one tutor. Mickey sighed. Despite a general commitment to trickery and disappointment, there were occasions when chance and fate conspired to do you a favor. The last tutor standing was the cute girl with the blue ribbon. Something about her inspired deference even in Sister Angelica, who gestured to the seat beside Mickey and allowed the girl to walk and sit without any artificial impetus.

"Hello," Mickey managed to whisper, though his throat seemed opposed to obeying his orders. "I'm Mickey."

"Hello," Blue Ribbon said back. "My name's Carlie."

They shared the flicker of a smile.

School had just become Mickey's favorite place.

CHAPTER 7

Welcome to the West, Mister

Mort took two kitchen knives and laid them on the burner. It would take a moment before they were red hot, and the delay irritated him. This had become his daily routine in the five years since his mother died, but he still had not developed any patience for the delays.

"Shalla," he whispered between clenched teeth, recalling the name of the Stanford researcher who had dosed him with LSD. He picked up one of the knives and struck the burner with the heating blade. A shower of sparks flew over the rusty range.

A small TV Mort had on his kitchen table began playing the opening refrain of The Partridge Family, the new hit from the 1970 fall line-up. Mort didn't wait for the opening animation of the bird emerging from an egg. He reached over and pulled his JVC, which had been designed to look like a space helmet, away from the wall hard enough to rip the cord from the outlet with a spark. Still not content, he launched the TV into the bathroom, where it landed with the crash of broken glass.

Mort had taken to working at the docks. But even a shift of grueling labor wasn't enough to quell his ever present anger. He'd go home to lift weights when he'd finished work for the day. Now 23, he'd packed 215 pounds onto his six-foot-three frame.

The knife blades finally turned red, and Mort set a chunk of hash the size of a diamond between them and pressed the glowing metal together. He leaned over and inhaled the creamy smoke. Standing back to his full height, he felt his balance slipping. He staggered two steps backward, bumped into his refrigerator, and slid down to the floor. The impact of his body against the appliance dislodged a paper which floated down and landed on his lap, but Mort didn't notice as his chin had already come to rest against his chest. Briefly, his anger subsided as he slept, but was never extinguished; instead, it hibernated like a feral beast.

***

When Mort awoke, the first thing he saw was the paper in his lap. He ground his knuckles into his eyes and lifted the item for a closer look. It was a newspaper clipping from the *Boston Daily Register*. How had he managed to get his hands on that while living here in California? He put his fingers against his throbbing skull and tried to remember. A voice he couldn't be sure was his own whispered in the back of his mind, "*You found it in a shipping crate. Read.*"

"What do I care about some piece of trash," Mort said aloud.

"*Read!*" The voice insisted.

Mort shook his head and tried to focus on the text. The article was about a strangely talented young girl. Through bleary eyes, Mort read the opening words, but after a few lines he sat up straight with new purpose. The story said the mother of the talented girl was named Shalla, and the article indicated she'd been a Stanford grad student.

"Shalla," Mort whispered, grinding the newsprint with his thumb. His eyes drifted to the by-line. "Ruth Nooker." There was even a headshot. Mort glanced at his front door and was surprised to see a trail of his old friend, the black smoke, beckoning him. He hadn't seen the smoke for a while, not since the day his mother was killed. He regarded it now with a melancholy smile. "Boston," Mort whispered.

The scent of the hash still lingered in the kitchen, and in the numbing respite from his overpowering rage, Mort had a flash of clarity. He had no money, but his time with the Hell's Angels had taught him how to extract what he needed from those around him. There were always evil men with full pockets against whom he could test his strength. He looked forward to the challenge. Resolved, Mort lifted himself from the floor, crumpled the paper into his pocket, and headed out the door.

***

Mort rode the ferry to Sausalito and stuck out his thumb on Highway 101, accepting the first ride from a long haul trucker pulling out of a coffee and eggs place on the main drag. As the big red rig lurched through the traffic on Main Street toward the open road, Mort took a look at the roofs of Sausalito, which were little rectangles speckled in and out of the forested hillside above the town center. His permanent LSD tickertape made them appear as letters in an alphabet he could not decipher, but he was struck by a feeling that he would return someday to the city and those roofs.

The trucker was headed for Sacramento, then I-80, and finally Salt Lake City. They didn't speak much as they made their way, but Mort didn't get a sense of wrongdoing from the driver so he had no inclination to separate him from his property. The driver let Mort off with a smile and a wave outside the Bonneville Flats, never knowing how close to violent misfortune he'd come. A half hour later, a young guy in a heavy duty dual wheel pickup pulled over, rolled down the passenger window and called out, "I'm going to Casper." Mort got in and was momentarily nonplussed when he saw that the kid was a lefty. Mort had nothing against lefties, but it meant the kid could steer with his right while comfortably aiming the nasty-looking revolver he rested in his lap—a .44 from the look of it—at Mort's kidney. "Welcome to the West, mister," the kid said, with a smile that suggested the gun was just a means of practical self-preservation and nothing at all malicious. "Behave yourself and we'll get along fine."

Mort feared nothing except his own personal demons and the few humans who seemed to sense his true psychic identity. You could never tell what powers were held by others with the sight. No one else could intimidate him but he was also a practical man and knew that a hole in the side of his rib cage would put a serious dent in his hopes of finding those responsible for the mess his life had become. He settled back and decided to enjoy the ride and rob someone else farther down the road. As the kid put the truck in gear and rolled forward in first, the vehicle began to shake. Mort looked over. "I think you got transmission problems, kid."

"Hah! Guess I surprised you. That's just Scorpio."

"What's Scorpio?" Mort looked back. There was a giant kennel in the back of the pickup and it was rocking so hard that the truck frame shimmied. He could see a giant foaming mouth biting at the grate, trying to get out. Mort was interested.

"My dog," the kid said. "I had a girlfriend. She liked this mythology, you know, so I named him after one of those zodiac symbols called Scorpio. It's one of those bugs with pincers and a stinger. Scorpio's the best kind of a mix; mostly German Shepherd but a little bit of Pyrenees in him. That's what makes him so damn big. Those Basque sheepherders use the Pyrenees dogs to guard against wolves and varmints and such."

"What's a Basque?"

"You know, they come from another country. They're good with sheep and mountains and such. That dog there, he's too mean so they give him to me. He kills everything, but I like 'im. I whip 'im pretty good and he's afraid of me, but a guy like you, why, he'd pull your arm right off."

The kid kept talking and Mort learned to more or less tune it out. The ride would have worked out fine for the kid if he had not been in the mood to pick up stranded sojourners. Outside of Thermopolis, he stopped for an older man wearing torn bib blue jeans with no underwear from the look of it, no shirt, and a stars and stripes bandana. His stringy gray ponytail hung long off his back. Mort knew the type. This guy must have burned all his bridges in Haight-Ashbury and was headed back to Ann Arbor, or New York. The bedraggled fellow opened the door, climbed up and hopped on the bench seat, jostling Mort.

"Scoot over!" he howled, snapping the order like he was making a joke, but also meaning it.

Mort frowned and moved over. He had a gun barrel touching his left hip and a smelly hippie pushing against his thigh on the right. He was on the verge of combustion when the hippie saved him the trouble. The old boy reached into his bib pockets and fished around, a pretty good pantomime of looking for something that Mort knew was not there in the first place. The newcomer let out a long sigh like the hiss of air coming out of a tire. He put on a glum look and turned to ask Mort a question, but the thousand yard stare on Mort's face made him think better of it. He sat back, reconsidered, and leaned forward again. He reached across Mort's broad chest, oblivious to the gun, and tapped the driver on the shoulder.

"Hey, buddy. You holdin'?"

The kid worked his lips but no words came out. He closed his mouth, stared ahead and kept driving. The hippie repeated himself. No answer from anyone. It might have ended there, but the old boy had to signify his dissatisfaction. As he leaned back, he murmured, "Thanks a lot. Jackass."

DAN WOLL & WALTER RHEIN

The kid turned his head to Mort. "What'd he say?" as if the bedraggled hitcher was not even in the cab.

"He asked you if you're holding and then he called you a jackass."

"What the hell does that mean?"

"A jackass is a kind of—"

"Don't play with me! I know damn well what a jackass is. What am I supposed to be holding?"

"He wants to know if you have any dope."

The kid slammed on the brakes. The pickup fishtailed. He let up to straighten it out and braked again, throwing the unbelted and unsuspecting passengers against the dash. Twice.

"I got no need for drug-dealing scum. Get the hell out, commie!"

The hitcher protested, "Who's talking drugs? I just wanted a little marijuana."

The young man had recently heard a lecture on this from his Missouri Synod pastor. He snapped, "That's a gateway drug and this here's the gateway to the high desert for you. Now get out!"

He lifted his hand, and for the first time the hippie realized there was a weapon in the truck. The old boy jumped out and started up the road. As he walked away, he turned back and gave them the finger. The enraged kid let out the clutch too fast and killed the truck. The hitchhiker gave a worried glance back, stepped off the road a few feet and picked up the pace.

There was something wrong with the truck's ignition system and it took a few tries before the engine caught. When it did, the kid winked at Mort. "That bum needs a scare. Watch this, y'all." He stepped on the gas and the truck lurched ahead.

"I'm gonna come so close to him, he'll dirty his drawers." It was Mort's turn to have an idea. The gun was no longer a factor in this redneck cybernetics. The kid was locked in on a target path that would take him a few inches off the hitchhiker's left shoulder. Just as he jounced off the road to brush the old man, Mort grabbed the wheel and pulled it to the right.

There was a sickening thud.

"What'd you do?" the kid cried. "What'd you do?"

He slammed on the brakes, put the truck in neutral, and hopped out with the motor still running. The impact had thrown the old bohemian twenty feet up the road. As the kid ran to him, Mort slid behind the steering wheel.

The kid turned around to scream something, but stopped short when he saw Mort bend down in the cab to release the parking brake. Mort revved up the engine to a roar and engaged the clutch. The truck leaped forward. The kid stood up, but by then the truck was on him, and then, over him. Mort looked in the rearview mirror and saw two clumps of denim, boots, and a torn cowboy hat. He backed up until he felt the pickup's big dual wheels bump. The next sound was a muffled scraping of something being dragged on the undercarriage. The scraping stopped as the truck continued backward. Several lumps of denim appeared in front of the truck. Mort got out, walked over and examined the carnage. It was not easy to sort the blue jean pockets from the rest of the mess, but he did. What he found surprised him. The kid had five bucks in his pocket and some toothpicks. The old man had squirreled away seven hundred dollar bills and a bunch of tens in his can of chew.

There was a tarp in the back of the truck. Mort wrapped up the biggest body parts he could find and dragged the bundle away from the road and into a dry gulch. He threw a few rocks on the tarp to hold things down. He had almost returned to the truck when he thought of something. He retraced his steps, uncovered the bodies and fished around for awhile but didn't find the gun. He stood up and looked at the big red sun settling among purple clouds. He scratched his head and said, "Damn. Welcome to the West, boys."

He went back to the truck and as he opened the cab door, he saw what he was looking for under the truck's rocker panel. The kid must have dropped the gun out of his lap when he got out in a panic. Next to where the gun had fallen there was also a plastic bag of Polaroids. The Polaroids were of naked girls who looked too young and too miserable to be having their picture taken voluntarily. The bag gave Mort a queasy feeling and he tossed it far into the desert.

Mort considered. Almost eight hundred dollars, a truck, and a gun. It was a good day's work. There was one more thing. The dog. He didn't need a dog, especially one so huge and noisy. He climbed up in the back of the pickup and let the tailgate down. He took the kid's gun and checked the barrel. All the cylinders showed copper bullet heads. Six shots ready to go. He held it out and pulled the trigger.

Bam!

The recoil was a satisfying reassurance that the gun worked. He had no particular interest in killing the dog, but if he let it out and it turned on him, he was ready. If it ran, it was big enough to fend for itself. He opened the kennel door, expecting an explosion of fur and paws and a mad scramble for the ground. Instead, the dog stuck its nose out, looked around at Mort and whimpered.

"Come on, boy! Git!"

Mort shook the cage. The dog retreated. Daylight was burning and he had to get going. He pushed the kennel to the edge of the tailgate and tipped it over. The biggest dog he had ever seen hopped out and landed gracefully, but instead of bolting, it lay down, tongue out, looking at Mort. The animal low-crawled over to Mort's feet and paused. A jackrabbit crossed the road behind them. Scorpio exploded and in a burst of speed was on the rabbit and shaking it to death. Then he brought it back and laid it at Mort's feet.

"Well, I guess you're a killer," Mort said. "That makes two of us. Why dontcha' come along for the ride?" He opened the cab and Scorpio hopped in and sat proudly in the passenger seat.

CHAPTER 8

The Scary Cowboy

Every day at St. Asors there was a test. Anyone who got less than seven out of ten correct needed tutoring. Mickey was usually half decent in arithmetic, but after meeting his tutor he made sure to get at least five wrong every day. Carlie sat down next to Mickey and showed him his mistakes. After thirty minutes, the eighth graders trooped out. The room got darker. The sun had been taken away.

The next day they took the test again. Mickey only managed four correct answers. This time, he was sent out into the hallway with the tutor. To abate the scandal of a girl and boy tutoring pair, the nuns forbade any speech that wasn't related to mathematics. It didn't matter. Mickey's tongue would have tied itself into a knot at any attempt to express the complexity of his feelings. The fact that such an effort was forbidden imbued a heartrending beauty to the words that would forever remain unspoken. Lancelot and Guinevere could hardly have wished for a more tragic predicament.

Carlie didn't seem to mind that the more coaching Mickey received, the worse he seemed to do. As he pretended to struggle with math, she leaned in so close that Mickey could hear her breathe. Once, her hair touched his crew cut forehead and it was as if his whole body went numb and came alive with electricity all at once. He could smell the Luster Crème shampoo in her hair. She could smell the Brylcreme on his. His normal shyness melted away under her warm gaze. She looked at him and something passed between the two that Mickey wouldn't ever fully understand.

The process repeated daily for a glorious week.

It didn't take the nuns that much longer to figure out something was amiss. The shy courting came to a screeching halt when Sister Alice came up behind the two and saw the look that was passing between them. There was no tutoring going on. She grabbed Mickey's little patron saint of addition by the back of her jumper and hustled her off.

"You are to get back to your room right now," she admonished Carlie before turning to Mickey. "And you, young man, are to stay after school and memorize pages four and five of the catechism. Both the questions and the answers."

Mickey would have rather had the ruler beating.

The nuns had no place to go. They could stay all day. Those student inmates sentenced to the dreaded memorization detail could not leave until they had it all locked down. It was 5:30 p.m. by the time Mickey committed the pages to memory and rushed home.

***

Monday morning came, and in marched a new tutor, Gene Torino. The kids knew and feared the older boys. It was the older boys' job to chase the younger students around and terrorize them three times a day at every recess.

Gene was the biggest, meanest kid in school. There was a rumor that his dad was in the Mafia. He sat down beside Mickey and said, "If you fail this test, you should hope to die before I kill you for fun."

Mickey never failed another addition quiz. He thought about failing on purpose to see if they would send his girlfriend back, but he was afraid he would get Gene again. He was even more afraid at the possibility that he might, somehow, get his angel in trouble. Mickey was starting to understand what the feelings were. He felt heroic. And sad.

Every now and then he would see Carlie in the lunchroom, or their eyes would meet as they passed in the hallway, girls walking in one unisex line, and boys parallel to them in another. The nuns were big on lines. The two children started to develop a code of winking and blinking to acknowledge their bond, whatever it was.

Then she disappeared.

She wasn't in the halls, she wasn't at the cafeteria, she was nowhere Mickey had learned he could catch a quick glimpse of her. At first, Mickey assumed she must have gone on vacation, but deep down he knew something terrible had happened. Her absence grew to a week, then a month, then several months and she still failed to appear.

Mickey didn't see Carlie at school again, except once.

Instead of a lawn, there was a yard of alligatored asphalt in front of the building. Within that yard, there were several giant oak trees. Around the base of the trees, there was a gap between the trunk and the asphalt like the bergshrund crevasse where a glacier pulls back from the foot of a mountain. These moats would fill up with water when it rained.

Mickey had occupied himself with the task of building a bridge out of Popsicle sticks, squatting like a monkey in blue pants, when a car pulled up alongside the fenced-in playground. A tingle at the back of Mickey's neck told him something crazy was happening. Carlie got out of the car and Mickey's heart leaped, but she wasn't alone. Two women and a police officer accompanied her.

Mickey had never seen a police officer with a little kid in tow. The way the officer was looking around, it seemed his friend wasn't in trouble. On the contrary, the cop appeared to be guarding her. She walked by the oak tree and Mickey took a deep breath. She was not a big person to begin with but she must have lost a quarter of her weight. She was a skeleton. Tears were rolling down her sunken cheeks. The tears made her appear much younger.

Their eyes met. She looked like she wanted to say something, but her escorts kept her moving and gently prodded her into the building. Five minutes later, they came out holding two boxes containing her winter coat, some books and her lunch pail—a little metal box with a cheap handle on the top and colorful pictures of Snow White and her dwarfs on the side. It was the sum of everything a kid could possess at St. Asors.

As they exited, Carlie broke free to run over to Mickey. The grown-ups panicked, dropped the boxes and chased after her. She got to her friend first. She took his hand. Her eyes bored into Mickey, straight through to his soul.

"Watch out for the scary cowboy," she said in a rush, her voice trembling with terror. "He's—"

One of the women gently took hold of Carlie's arm above the elbow.

"Come on, honey. We need to get you to your new home."

CHAPTER 9

Is This You?

Mort had an uneventful drive stopping only for brief naps at public rest areas as he made his way to Boston. The first light of day struck the city as he arrived, and he navigated the winding streets of the sprawling metropolis stopping once to buy a map and once more to ask directions. It was early morning when he parked his truck across the street from the head offices of the *Boston Daily Register*. He scratched Scorpio behind the ear as he regarded the place. Mort had never had any love for newspapers. They were run by self-righteous privileged people with the kind of access to lawyers that allowed them to print anything they wanted—regardless of truth. More often than not, Mort or one of his friends had been portrayed as the wrongdoer in an altercation before any of the facts had been properly examined. Stories like that created a reputation that stuck even if the truth later came to light. Whole lives were shaped and then ruined by the careless words of indifferent college brats. Such abuse of power deserved punishment.

He switched off the engine but didn't bother to remove his keys. Scorpio could handle the truck. Giving the dog a final pat, he slid off the seat and stepped into the street, closing the door behind him. Scorpio moved over to take Mort's vacated seat. Mort smiled.

The smoke trail appeared in the air before him, and the lean biker walked to the front door. He kept his eyes focused on the other world, and he knew by doing so the blind would take no notice of him. Mort followed a reporter through the front door and into a large hall. There was a desk with a receptionist, but Mort didn't even give them the courtesy of a look.

Mort trailed the reporter for a few more steps until the smoke guided him to a recessed stairway. He turned and began to climb.

Three flights later, he emerged into a set of office cubicles. Most of the occupants of this room were engaged in work, so it took no great effort to influence them not to look up. The smoke continued to guide Mort to a filing cabinet, which he opened.

His fingers flicked along the files until he came to "N," and soon found what he was looking for: a manila folder with "Ruth Nooker" printed on the corner.

The first few documents were photocopies of restraining orders out on the reporter. Mort's eyes narrowed at the look of them. It seemed Ruth had a habit of hassling innocent people in order to get her scoops.

He flicked through a few more pages before finding a pay stub. He committed the address to memory and closed the file.

On the way out, one woman did look at him and pause as she walked down the hall.

Mort winked at her.

The woman looked down and hurried away.

***

Ruth Nooker was startled by the sound of a knock on her door. The impact was that of the heel of a clenched fist rather than a knuckle, and the pauses between the blows were slow and deliberate.

Ruth stood up from her couch and crept toward the door to peer out the peephole. Her blood ran cold. She hadn't expected that the raw-boned muscular biker with the club foot might one day turn up on her doorstep. She remembered him dancing that night in L.A., the night that woman was killed.

"I can hear the TV," the young man said.

Ruth was silent.

"I know you're standing behind the peephole, it went dark."

Ruth tried to steady herself and regain control of the situation. She checked the security chain, took a deep breath, and opened the door. Would he recognize her?

"Can I help you?"

The man held up a crumpled newspaper clipping.

"Ruth Nooker?"

"Oh, I'm sorry," Ruth replied, "I think you have the wrong house."

The man smiled cool and deadly, never taking his eyes off her.

"Believe me, I have ways of knowing. I don't have the wrong house," he said. "I got this address from your office."

Ruth clenched her jaw. "They would never have given out the address of a reporter."

"I didn't say they 'gave it to me,' I said I 'got it.'"

It took a moment for that to sink in, and when it did the color drained from Ruth's face.

"This is what's going to happen. I'm going to come in, and we're going to have a conversation. This conversation is very important. You can either open your door or have me knock it down."

Ruth said nothing. She began to push the door closed. Whether she intended to remove the chain or turn the dead bolt, her action never came to pass. There was the sound of flesh striking wood, followed by the howl of a screw yanked from a wooden frame, then the door came flying back to strike her in the face. Ruth crumpled in a wad in her entryway, a trickle of blood running down her nose.

The man entered and leaned the door back against its frame behind him so that, from the street, it looked still to be in place. He kneeled, and lifted the security chain to show her.

"These things are worse than worthless," he said, "because they make you feel safe when you are not." He tossed the chain aside. "My name's Mort."

Ruth lost consciousness.

***

When Ruth came to, she was duct-taped by the ankles, wrist, and body to a solid oak chair. For a moment she thought her captor was gone, and in a desperate convulsion she rocked and tipped over. Hitting the ground hurt. She started to cry as Mort stepped back into the kitchen.

"Do you prefer the floor? That's fine; I've spent a few nights down there myself."

Mort pulled out the clipping again.

"Tell me more about Shalla Stillman, and her husband Alan, and their daughter Carlie." Mort fixed Ruth with an intense look, and suddenly stiffened. For a terrifying moment, he sat utterly still, but then his body began to tremble as if he were receiving an electric shock. His eyes darted left and right, and Ruth whimpered in terror.

Then the young biker shook himself and fixed the bound reporter with a stare so intense there could be no doubt he was back in full control of his faculties.

"You were there," he said, "I remember you."

"I was," Ruth replied, "I remember you too, and your mother."

Mort snarled like an animal and lunged.

"Do you think you were the only one who lost something that night?" Ruth cried. "I've been investigating that incident for years. Shalla Stillman took out a restraining order against me and tried to get me expelled rather than accept any responsibility for her involvement. She flat out refuses to respond to any inquiry. There wasn't even an official investigation; the government covered it up. Powerful people are involved ... secrets..."

Mort leaned back. "I assure you, she'll answer to me. Do you have an address?"

Ruth hesitated. "Will you let me go?"

"That's a yes," Mort replied, "give it to me."

Ruth began to sob, but she gave the address.

"Thank you, you've been very helpful, Ruth."

"Please let me go."

"I can't, little lady. You'll tell."

"No! I won't. I promise. Please."

"I'm truly sorry, Ruth, but all I can do is promise that you'll feel less pain than my ma. But be assured that the ones responsible for this will be punished too."

***

Two hours later, Mort walked out of the woods to the north of Walden Pond, hands and pants stained with dirt. The folks with restraining orders out against Ruth Nooker wouldn't be hassled anymore. A comforting cloud enveloped Mort, and he felt soothed and renewed.

Mort climbed back into his truck absently scratching Scorpio as he put it in gear. The address Ruth had given was up in Watertown; a short, 20 minute drive away.

As the highway rolled beneath him, Mort settled into a dark meditation. He felt the smoke coalesce around him in something close to a comforting embrace. There was a certain electricity in the air, a pregnant anticipation, a sense that a wrong would soon be made right.

Darkness fell as Mort drove past the nondescript yellow house that served as the residence for the Stillman family. Mort reduced his speed to a slow roll and gave the home a glare before driving off to find a dark street to park and catch some sleep until dawn. In the morning, he got a paper, and found a rental house a few blocks down from the Stillmans. He stayed inside for a month, acclimating himself to the energy of his surroundings. The closer he got to them, the more he felt the presence of his mother. He sometimes wondered if she was tormented wherever she was. The thought agitated him.

Walking past the Stillman house with Scorpio, he met her.

The young girl stood in her yard in a white dress, a blue ribbon tied in her hair. The sight of the girl startled Mort. He instantly knew she had the sight. As small and weak as she appeared, he knew she could gaze right through him. Mort did not scare easily, but he felt a bead of sweat form on his neck and roll down his back.

Scorpio, sensing his master's elevated emotion, began to growl.

"I like your blue ribbon," Mort said. "My mother used to wear a ribbon like that."

The girl did not reply, but Mort felt an intrusion on his psyche. Was she reaching out?

Your mother is dead, isn't she?

The girl had not moved; what power did she have? With growing frustration, Mort pulled the newspaper clipping from his pocket.

"Is this you?" he asked, clutching the paper in his hand and holding it forth in accusation.

Scorpio began to lunge, but Carlie did nothing.

Why are you here? came a voice in Mort's mind.

"What's going on here?" said a voice echoing not in his mind but in the real world. Mort looked up to see Carlie's dad approaching. A few more words were exchanged and Mort managed to pull Scorpio away, but not before Carlie hit him with a psychic jolt that sent him reeling. As Mort shuffled off back to his rental, he felt deeply disturbed, as if his soul had been raked and trampled upon.

Back at the rental, Mort took a tab of acid and placed it on his tongue. He let out a breath deep enough to allow what was left of his soul to escape, and plunged backward onto his mattress and down seven fathoms.

As always, any kind of peace was hard to come by, but then he fantasized about watching the Stillman family burn, and that provided enough relief to let sleep take him.

CHAPTER 10

The Departure

Carlie watched the strange man haul his belongings out of the rental unit and pile them in a truck. He carried box after box, never looking up, though Carlie was aware he knew she was watching. When he was finished, he dusted off his hands, put his key under the mat, and climbed into his vehicle. The truck took one last slow roll down the street in front of Carlie's house before accelerating around the corner and off toward parts unknown. Her mother and father stood beside her, and with the departure of the strange man, the tension lines that had taken up permanent residence around Shalla's eyes eased.

"I'm glad he's gone," Shalla said, "maybe we'll get a chance to have some peace now."

Alan said nothing.

The rest of the day passed with moribund reflection rather than jubilation. The Stillman family spoke to each other in low whispers as if not daring to provoke the eerily calm universe. The more time passed without incident, the more they all began to relax. Carlie went to bed still aware of a strange tension in the atmosphere, but encouraged by the fact that it seemed to be dissipating.

In the middle of the night, Carlie woke to the sound of whistling; a sad melody that seemed familiar as if someone had taken a pop song and put it in a minor key.

Carlie didn't move, but she opened her eyes and sought shapes in the bleary darkness. The whistling continued and Carlie did her best to place the direction of the sound. In a moment, she realized the noise came from beneath her.

Carlie slept on the first floor because she was the youngest and the first floor had the smallest bedroom. Her brother and her parents had bigger rooms upstairs. Orienting on the whistling, Carlie slipped the covers off her body and slid to the edge of her bed. Though she moved as carefully and as quietly as possible, the whistling stopped instantly.

With greater urgency but as much stealth as she could muster, Carlie got out of bed and walked into the hallway. Every part of her wanted to go up and alert her parents. The sense of impending danger surged in her psyche. Carlie felt the need to reach behind her and close the door to her room.

Time slowed. Carlie closed her eyes. Deep beneath the fear alarm that was sounding throughout her nervous system, she could detect a sound. The sound repeated over and over in a steady rhythm; it was something she sensed rather than heard, but she never questioned that the noise might be a figment of her imagination. She knew with absolute conviction that the noise was all too terribly real.

Tick, tick, tick.

Understanding hit Carlie and she drove toward the front door of her house just as the room exploded behind her. The shockwave caught her from behind and sent her flying down the hall. She hit the floor and slid; the impact rattled her perception, but the slide kept her alive.

Her consciousness blurred and she couldn't be sure if she'd lost awareness for a moment. Dimly, she saw a flash of something at the fringes of her vision and realized after a moment that they must be flames. Flames surrounded her. Carlie breathed in smoky air. She could hear a pounding.

Who was pounding?

Where was she?

She tried to lift herself onto her knees, but failed. She crawled, away from the heat, toward the front door. The sound of pounding got louder and louder and finally the door broke down.

"Carlie!"

Carlie looked up. It was John, her neighbor. He lifted his forearm to his face and reached down for Carlie. Carlie suddenly became aware that the heat she'd felt only dimly before was overwhelming.

"Dad," she said, "Mom, Robert!"

John grabbed Carlie and retreated toward the door.

"We have to get them," Carlie said, her dizziness pierced by adrenaline and fear. "They'll be burned, they're upstairs!"

"We can't get them, Carlie!" John replied, reaching the door and pulling her out into the cool night.

"We have to!"

Outside, she saw the flames licking upward like a hungry animal. The house was enveloped. John had taken a great risk just to kick in the front door.

"Mom, Dad, Robert!" Carlie cried.

John held her back.

The sound of sirens and spraying water couldn't drown out the laughing crackle of the flames.

Carlie dropped to her knees and sobbed.

Nobody else made it out.

***

The next few days were chaos.

The police determined that an explosive device had been planted in an area of the crawl space directly beneath Carlie's bed. There were no fingerprints or any other clues.

Carlie tried to tell the cops about the cowboy with the dog, but whenever she brought up his description, their eyes glazed over as they listened without hearing. The police refused to take any notes about her mysterious visitor. She pleaded with them again and again until she became hysterical.

"Why won't you listen?" she howled, pounding her fists against the chests of the investigators stopping only when exhaustion compelled her to silence. Larger forces were at play; she was too little to understand, so she had no other recourse than sullen acceptance.

Her life became not her own, and the next few months were a blur. Her grandmother had passed away years ago and Shalla and Alan had no other relatives. Carlie was placed in a foster home, but she was too withdrawn to engage. They sent her back. Carlie had said nothing since her failed interview with the police. Back at the office, Carlie managed to utter her first words: "St. Asors."

Her coordinating officer looked at her with surprise.

"I left my things at St. Asors," Carlie said, "I need to go back for them. I have a picture of my family in my locker."

Carlie worked up some tears, but they weren't sincere. Her emotions were numb, her insides were numb. She remembered how people were supposed to behave, and she'd recovered enough to be able to fake it. In truth, her possessions meant nothing to her; she wanted to talk to the boy.

The boy who could see like she could.

The officer gathered Carlie up and took her along with two police officers to the school, where Carlie managed to give them the slip for a desperate, whispered message.

Job completed, Carlie submissively accompanied her guardians as they placed her with her next family. Carlie made sure to smile and call the woman "Mom" and the father "Dad." She acquiesced to their will when it served her purpose, and resisted only after careful consideration.

CHAPTER 11

The Aftermath

The smoke guided Mort to the explosives. For the first time in his life, he had the sense that he was outside his own body and simply observing an act of nature. He saw his hands before him, but they seemed to act of their own volition. He found himself in a dark warehouse lifting a crate, then he was in his truck, then he was affixing a timer and detonation device.

On more than one occasion throughout the process, he caught himself whistling. He tried to stop, but the second his attention got diverted the whistling was back. After a while he gave up, and simply made an effort to lower the volume.

The crate fit perfectly into the crawl space. He could feel her above the spot he picked. The timer had already been set. Mort flipped the switch, crawled away and let the smoke take the wheel. Scorpio slept beside him, emitting a low, rumbling growl.

***

Mort did not witness the explosion. He was in his car and down the road before the timer went off. He knew the effort had been successful, the smoke told him so. A sense of calm like nothing he'd ever known descended upon him. It was as if the volume had been turned down on the world. He watched the reflective lights pass on the side of the road in perfect symmetry and felt at peace.

With the dawn came a longing to be near water.

The highway hummed, his mind didn't race, his skull did not compress upon his brain. He wondered if maybe, just maybe, his mother's soul was content at last.

He read about the explosion at interstate truck stops. A 'drifter' was mentioned as a prime suspect, but the paper was vague. It seemed the lady the man had been renting from made a positive identification on every mug shot they had.

"What do you think, Scorpio?" Mort asked, scratching the ears of his friend as he read the paper. "It seems to me the average person can't see through smoke."

Mort laughed, and Scorpio perked up his ears because it was the first time he'd heard his master make that sound.

"There are witness reports of a dog as well," Mort continued, "listen to this: a brown dog, a white dog, a spotted dog, a big dog, a small dog ... why, they mention every possible type of dog there is."

Scorpio yawned.

For a few days the high continued, and, almost, the smoke seemed to part. It was as if the interruption in his life had been bridged, and now reality could resume.

What possibilities awaited him? Mort found himself daydreaming on themes he'd never before dared to imagine.

If he'd continued into the wilderness and left the world behind as he intended, the story might have ended there. But at a rest stop outside of Gary, Indiana, Mort picked up a day-old newspaper with a headline he'd previously overlooked. "Watertown, Mass. Child Survives Terrible Blast."

Mort felt the color drain from his face. His growing sense of stability was jerked away from him in an instant.

She had survived?

How had he not known?

How had she deceived the smoke?

With shaking hands, Mort lowered the paper and found his great strength had drained from his legs. He stumbled to a bench and sat, reflecting.

What power did she have?

What else could she influence?

Mort lifted his hands to his eyes and fell into a kind of hibernation. The clouds seemed to accelerate above him, the sun raced across the sky, and the darkness closed in. The crushing sense returned; the constant, chronic agony in his mind—worse now as a result of his brief reprieve. It came slowly at first, gradually increasing with every passing second, an ongoing irritation that promised to become fatal after antagonizing him for decades.

By the time Mort had refortified himself enough to continue, it was two a.m. The rest stop was empty. Mort was startled to discover he could hear Scorpio barking in the parking lot. The barks were followed by the sound of breaking glass. Mort pushed open the door to the rest area and was just in time to see three muscular men opening the door of his truck. Again, Mort's body moved without his conscious command. He stood and walked deliberately toward the thieves.

Two were in the truck going through his things, while Scorpio barked madly in his steel kennel. The biggest one stood outside on guard, leaning on the hood with one foot up on the bumper. He barely stirred when he saw Mort approach. He spit out chewing tobacco and said, contemptuously, "Be cool, hillbilly, we'll be done in a minute. Hey, boys, hurry up, the owner needs his car."

The guy had jacked enough vehicles in his years to learn most people wouldn't risk a fight. He was a big guy and could have had a shot at defending himself if he had bothered to stand and square up, but his confidence was such that he chose to relax even further, bending his head back to let out a loud horselaugh to the empty Indiana sky.

He chose poorly.

Mort grabbed him by the throat. The car-jacker had time to sense that he had opened up a different can of peaches by antagonizing the tall stranger, but it was too late. Mort banged the thief's head violently against the hood of the car a half dozen times. The other two came out the back panel doors in time to see the lifeless body of their friend slump to the pavement. Mort might have had a case for self-defense if he had let it go at that, but his rage was insatiable. He lunged like a wolf and grabbed the second thief by his ponytail. The third guy ran and was never seen again. Ponytail barked out in panic, "Hey, man, enough. We give up."

Mort's free pass with the law ran out just then. The state trooper who had pulled up behind the fracas hopped out in time to hear the plea.

"Everybody! Freeze!"

Mort ignored him and bent his opponent to the ground by yanking mercilessly on his ponytail.

The cop said, "Stop!"

Mort slugged Ponytail into unconsciousness with a crushing blow before the trooper started in on Mort. The trooper wasn't supposed to be carrying a blackjack, but he'd been on the force long enough to know it was worth risking a reprimand to have one. He got lucky with his first blow to the back of Mort's head which dazed the lean biker. It still took several more strikes to render the man unconscious.

At the trial, Mort had some concern about the history of his truck. But he smiled when he found out the vehicle had been reported stolen over a year before. That meant there was nothing to connect him to the two bodies he'd left wrapped in a tarp in the desert. But Ponytail didn't survive, and the trooper's testimony got Mort ten years.

Scorpio was put down.

CHAPTER 12

High School

The passage of years could not make Mickey forget Blue Ribbon. Her portrait hung in a position of prominence in his memory. But though treasured, her features slowly became part of the background; viewed daily but rarely seen. Until, at last, some subconscious part began to wonder if perhaps he had imagined her from nothing.

Mickey's sophomore year began under the somber cloud of Nixon's resignation, but that didn't stop him, like most boys, from becoming inclined toward the pursuit of parties, drinking, and general hell-rousing.

His talent of calling quarters persisted, and even began to manifest in different ways. Mickey still mostly heeded Curly's advice not to discuss such things, but sometimes his suspicions would slip out disguised as casual philosophy, or teenage wonderment.

Mickey had a friend named William who was always willing to push the envelope a level or two beyond what Mickey found comfortable. That inclination was probably the main reason they were friends. One weekend William's parents were away, William talked some older kids into buying them beer. A small crowd of guys and girls headed out to White's Pond, where they drank, danced, and capped things off with a spontaneous swim. The girls were hard to convince at first, but Mickey could be brilliant at times.

"Underwear is the same as a swimming suit," he managed, and the group was inclined to be persuaded so the logic stuck.

It should have been enough for any of them, but William could never just flirt with fate; no, he had to round the bases, lure disaster into his car, and go howling off in a cloud of dust, hell bent on chaos, glory, or both.

"Breakfast at my house!" William cried. It was pitch dark and they were riled up on rock 'n' roll and Rolling Rock by the time they arrived.

"Mickey," William said, "I don't have a key to the front door. Run around to the back, come through the house and let everybody in. I don't want anyone getting killed in the darkness."

Still charged from his first experience with coed midnight swimming, Mickey only gave a passing thought to the question of who was going to be killed, and by whom? He took off at a run through the alley, threw open the back door and charged into the dark landing.

Except, there was no floor.

Instead, there was an unguarded stairway to the basement three feet in. William thought that Mickey knew. Mickey didn't know anything except that he was flying into darkness. Suddenly, William's cryptic warning about imminent death became all too clear.

But then, time slowed.

Mickey felt a stillness, stiller than night. A subconscious jolt triggered a physical response faster than thought. He adjusted as a cat would react when thrown off a rooftop. He felt lithe, agile, loose and hyper-aware as his hands shot forward as if guided toward the railing. His fingers closed around the smooth, rounded wood. Mickey felt as if he were hovering for a minute. As his hand stabilized him, his legs caught up to his torso and rotated under his body. Then Mickey was vertical, and his leading foot tapped a stair. The other foot followed and there he was, firmly planted on the step.

Mickey shook his head, disoriented by his return from hyper-reality. He had sensed the fall before it happened. He didn't know how, but he knew that he knew. It had been more than reflex; like something else had been in control. What was going on with him? The question left him deeply disturbed. He released the rail and made a fist to stop his hand from shaking.

He stumbled through the house and opened the door. The darkness hid the fact that Mickey's skin was as white as William's flashing grin.

"You didn't fall, did you?" William asked.

"No, but I should have."

William thought it was a joke and laughed.

***

As much as Mickey tried to ignore his special abilities, he couldn't deny that weird things were beginning to happen more often. Every now and then he tested the waters to see if he could talk with his friends about what he was experiencing, but no sooner would he start to lay the groundwork for his reveal than their eyes would glaze over and he'd lose his audience. Mickey didn't know if they were anticipating what he was going to say, or if some extrasensory power was drawing their interest away, but he became conditioned not to say anything.

Still, there were times when something got through and he inadvertently revealed himself, like the night the lights went out in Watertown.

It was Mickey's Junior year and he had a small part in the play. His mother had made him do it, selling him a line about how she'd never auditioned for the class play and that she'd always regretted it. So there Mickey was, stuck in a ridiculous suit and required to participate in a goofy song and dance number he was sure would end in disaster.

His friends were sure it would end in disaster too, that's why they all showed up right in the front row. Even from behind the curtain, Mickey could hear their whispered wisecracks and laughs.

Mickey sighed and wiped his brow.

A couple of the other dancers who had also been conscripted by their mothers threw him a sympathetic nod.

The music swelled and the stage-hand tensed, ready to pull the curtain, when suddenly, the lights went out.

Mickey was plunged so instantaneously into silence and darkness that he wondered if he'd passed out. But then he became aware of the gasp of the audience, and realized it was just the power that had gone. He stood for a second, reorienting himself, his mind hesitating between a place of dreams and the full reality he'd just been experiencing. The off-balance moment acted like a cosmic lightning rod.

"Mickey," said a girl's voice, "I need you to help me."

Mickey looked around, trying to identify the source of the voice.

"Did you hear that?" he asked the kid standing next to him.

"Hear what?"

About then, handheld lights began to appear behind the stage and in the audience. A few more minutes passed and the noises of the people sitting in silence became more restless and agitated. Mickey continued to glance around for the source of the unearthly voice. In his mind he saw her, angelic as ever, blue ribbon in her hair, but in his present reality there were only dark eyes.

Eventually, a teacher made his way to the stage.

"I'm sorry, folks, the thunderstorm has knocked out the power. We are going to have to cancel for tonight. Wait for our ushers with flashlights to guide you to the door, please."

There was a not too disappointed groan. It was only a school play and a matter of duty rather than anticipation. Some of the moms were fairly upset, but the dads were happy to get back to the bar.

Outside, Mickey met up with William and the others.

"Hey, Mickey," William said, "give us a couple dance moves. C'mon, we came all this way!" William was cackling as he said it.

Mickey smiled, but his bearing was serious.

"Guys, did you hear a girl's voice in the darkness?"

"What did she say?" William asked.

Mickey felt his cheeks flush, but the question was too important to drop.

"She said she needed my help."

"Oh yeah," William said, "I heard that, except it was your mother's voice and she was asking for my help." The quip elicited a round of laughter. Mickey punched William in the shoulder.

"I'm serious, I heard something in there."

"Yeah, but it was your grandmother," William continued, "but this time she was begging ... pleading ... Hahaha!"

"Seriously, man," Mickey said, "you want to bring my grandmother into this?"

But William couldn't catch his breath he was laughing so hard. "No wait ... no wait ... no wait," he was saying, wiping tears away. "It was ... it was ... it was ..."

"Shut up, I heard something. Did you see any girls in the crowd, any new girls?"

"Dude, it was dark, the lights were out, plus your grandmother and your mother were keeping me too busy to look around."

"Forget it!" Mickey said, turning away from his friends to take one final glance at the people emerging from the auditorium. Somehow, he knew the beautiful young girl with the blue ribbon in her hair wouldn't be there, but he looked anyway. He wondered if he would ever see her again. He hoped the voice, and the strain he had thought he'd heard, had been his imagination. He tried to push the thoughts aside, but concern settled down into the darkest corner of his mind and took up permanent residence.

CHAPTER 13

Gabby

It was late summer as Carlie walked down a quiet street in Palo Alto, California. Beneath her arm she carried a newspaper with an ad for a room circled in black ink. There were several more ads circled on the same page, some of them with large X's scribbled through them. It had been a long day.

Carlie made her way to the door of a quaint Tudor-style cottage with a manzanita bush hedge in front. She was Carlie Tillford now. The name change had come not due to marriage, but because she'd taken the last name of the foster family that had cared for her throughout her final years in high school. They hadn't elected to adopt her, because that would have been the end of the government checks, but the name change had pleased them and Carlie was in short supply of allies.

It served her to let the Tillfords think she'd changed her name out of appreciation, but that had not been the reason for the switch. It had been five years since the explosion that had killed her family and sometimes at night she could still see the image of the sidewalk outside her home blackened by the figure of the lean cowboy, standing like an animate shadow, brandishing a newspaper clipping about the talented Carlie Stillman. The camouflage of calling herself Tillford helped her sleep easier.

Carlie put the thoughts of her past aside, took a deep breath, and knocked on the door. A moment later an older, thin woman answered. She was in her seventies, but appeared remarkably fit. Her arms were taut with muscle, showing not a trace of slack skin on the biceps. Her knee-length skirt betrayed the athletic calves of a tennis player.

"Can I help you?" she said.

"Hello," Carlie replied, "I've come about the room." She held up the paper with the circled ad.

The woman's eyes narrowed.

"The ad specifies a grad student, a *responsible* grad student. How old are you?"

Carlie shifted her feet.

"I'm seventeen," she admitted.

"And you're attending Stanford?" The woman seemed skeptical, but there was something in her tone that betrayed a touch of intellectual curiosity.

"I had an accelerated course-load and earned a scholarship," Carlie replied, obviously giving the truncated answer.

"First in your class, I bet?" the woman replied.

Carlie gave a shy smile and nodded.

"OK," the woman replied, "why don't you come in and we can talk for a while?" She extended her hand. "My name is Madame Gabrielle LaJeunesse. I am a Professor of French Literature and any renter of mine will have to live without male visitors, TV, and especially," at this she dropped her voice, "no drugs."

Carlie nodded, affecting a respectful and submissive body language that pleased the older lady. Madame LaJeunesse led Carlie to a small kitchen and offered the young woman a chair.

"I'm sorry to have mentioned the drugs," Madame LaJeunesse said, "but so many of my Bacchanalian neighbors indulge in pharmaceutical retreats from reality that I would move if not for my sense of place in this cherished homestead. Ever since that author Ken Kesey began to frequent the area years ago, things have gone downhill. I don't know why dear Wallace put up with him."

"Wallace, Ma'am, I mean, Madame?" Carlie stuttered.

"Wallace Stegner, the shining light of our literary scene, my dear. He was their teacher. I don't know how he could tolerate them. Well, I suppose when you have read as many student essays as Wallace, even the flashes of basic competence that can be found among the scrawls of Kesey must inordinately sparkle. Anyway, enough of this, tell me about you." Madame LaJeunesse placed a cup of tea in front of Carlie, and then lifted up her own cup to stare at Carlie with discerning eyes.

Carlie took a deep breath. Although Madame LaJeunesse seemed strict, she couldn't completely hide a certain grandmotherly aspect that Carlie found appealing. Her days in foster care had accustomed Carlie to receiving affection at arm's length. In fact, she felt safest when the people around her kept at reasonable distance.

"I've been in state care since I was twelve," she began.

Madame LaJeunesse put her cup down as if realizing she was about to hear more than she had bargained for. She'd been teaching long enough to have heard every made up hard-luck story under the sun. As a result, she had developed an ability to recognize a true hard-luck case when she saw it.

"My parents died," Carlie continued, "my older brother too." She paused to take a sip of her tea, taking advantage of the moment to quell the emotions that suddenly welled up inside her. Madame LaJeunesse waited patiently, not speaking or moving so as to avoid infringing upon the young woman's need to collect herself. The older woman's presence soothed Carlie and after a brief pause the young woman was able to continue her story.

"I bounced around a couple foster homes until I ended up with the Tillfords. At that point, things stabilized enough so I could get through school. I really am just here to study, Madame. I can understand how you would be wary about having a stranger in your home. I don't feel I can protect myself yet, and it would be nice to have somebody ... not watching out for me ... but aware that if I don't come home some night, something is wrong."

At that point, the stern Professor of French Literature spontaneously reached over and placed her hand over that of the young girl.

"Say no more, child," Madame LaJeunesse said, "you've been through enough, I think. I can provide you with a safe and nurturing intellectual environment. After a story like yours, how could I not?"

Carlie found herself wiping away a tear. Her feelings told her this was a fortuitous meeting.

***

An unlikely friendship formed between the young girl and the reclusive landlord. Carlie spent hours in the library. In her scarce free time, she studied Tae-Kwondo and yoga. She eschewed parties and campus frivolities and lived a life even more severe than Madame LaJeunesse. In fact, Carlie was so studious that even the strict Madame began to suggest that there would be no harm if Carlie took "just a little time" for personal diversion.

"If you ever want to take a drive," Madame LaJeunesse said, "just let me know and you can borrow my Citroen. I hardly use it anyway as I prefer to walk to campus."

The warm and affectionate home had an effect on Carlie and she began to blossom into a beautiful woman. She attracted no shortage of suitors, but her brush with the lean biker and his dog had left her leery of men, except for one. Sometimes, late at night, she would think of Mickey with such intensity that the universe seemed to shake. She wondered if he still thought of her too. But he was a long way away and she hadn't talked to him since that stolen embrace and the whispers of warning at St. Asors.

At the end of a year, they had progressed to a point where Gabrielle insisted that Carlie call her "Gabby."

"Oh my, oh my," Gabby said, "I don't know what's coming over me! I have not allowed anyone to use that pet name of mine since I was a child."

They often had tea together in the early afternoon. Carlie began to reveal enough of herself that a mature and intelligent woman like Gabby could piece the rest together. But Gabby didn't push, allowing Carlie to emerge at her own speed.

They established a relationship of guarded intimacy, and there was never any question that Carlie would leave to move elsewhere. When she turned eighteen, Carlie gained control of a trust fund her parents had set up for her. Far from a fortune, the account was enough to ensure her living expenses would be covered as she set about preparing herself for the battles that lay ahead.

CHAPTER 14

Overcast

It was 1970 when Mort began his 10 year sentence, and the time passed slow like a kidney stone. Mort was indifferent to prison. Drugs were harder to come by and the company was nothing to brag about, but the law of the jungle applied and at that Mort had proven himself proficient. Early on, a couple of hopeful contenders tried to prove themselves by jumping the lean biker when they thought he wasn't aware.

They didn't know that Mort was *always* aware.

At the end of the fight, two men lay in puddles of their own blood, not moving on the cafeteria floor. Mort went to the feed line as if nothing had happened, and sat down quietly with his tray. The guards came a moment later, and saw blood on Mort's clothes.

"What happened to those two?" a guard said. It was Officer Parks, one of the older veterans who was smart enough to know there was no guarantee somebody else would come if he started something he couldn't finish. Parks maintained his position of authority, but not at the expense of basic human courtesy. That went a long way with Mort.

"How should I know?" Mort replied.

"There's blood on you."

"I tried to help," Mort said, in between bites of his food. The food was terrible, but it eased his hunger. He figured he'd better finish off his tray in case they decided to haul him off to solitary.

"But how did they get hurt?"

"I don't know, maybe they slipped and fell. There are plenty of health hazards around here."

Parks snorted, shook his head, and walked away.

Nobody else talked. Mort liked that about prison.

Two years into his sentence, Mort had an unexpected visitor. Parks again was called upon to handle Mort.

"Prisoner, come to the door and face the wall, hands behind."

Mort knew the drill. He stood and allowed himself to be cuffed. Even with hands behind his back he was dangerous, and he knew Parks knew. As a result, Parks didn't try any cheap shots and Mort didn't have to retaliate, so nobody got their skin split.

Mort knew where the visitation area was. He hadn't had any visitors, but he'd seen others go there. Parks walked him right by the visiting station without showing any signs of stopping. Mort tensed. Noticing the lean biker's muscles cord up, Parks offered an explanation.

"Easy, you've got a VIP visitor; this guy requested to see you face to face."

"Who is it?"

"I don't know, son. I'd guess government."

Mort nodded. He said nothing further but he felt the smoke coalesce about him. He wanted to be ready, and anything involving the government was the last thing he'd trust.

Parks opened a reinforced steel door with a small portal at the top and marched Mort in. Mort got to sit with his hands cuffed behind him, and in addition, Parks ran a chain to the table.

"VIP treatment, eh?" Mort growled.

"Hey, man, I just do what they tell me," Parks replied.

"Yeah, I've been compelled by a few voices myself."

Parks gave Mort a concerned look, but didn't reply. When Mort had been sufficiently restrained, Parks walked out. Mort kept his head down, but he heard Parks exchange a few mumbled words outside. A moment later, a man entered.

The man was tall and lean and wore a white lab coat. He was nearly bald, and what few hairs he did have were white. He had spectacles with circular lenses perched on his nose, and he reached up with uncomfortable frequency to itch behind his ear with a hard, jerking motion. Something about the man gave Mort a sense of the weight of history. It was as if this were a figure from a different place, a different time, who had stepped out of a history book and brought with him some cosmic trace of past horrors that would make even Mort recoil. A dark presence filled the space the two of them shared, and Mort was made uneasy.

"Mortimer LeFrance?" the man asked.

"Check the prisoner number," Mort replied. He thought he detected something of an accent in the man's speech. There was a sharpness in his voice, a shadow of something he had taken great pains to erase.

"My name is Doctor Martin. I regret to be the bearer of bad news—"

Mort cut him off.

"My father has died."

Dr. Martin nodded. "I I wasn't aware you knew."

"I didn't know, but what else could it be? Can I go now? I have some spring cleaning I want to finish up."

Dr. Martin ignored the quip and cleared his throat. "Your father..." he began, but the way he said 'father' startled Mort. It was drawn out, like 'fah-der.' Mort fixed the man with a piercing look.

"You a Kraut?"

The doctor recoiled. He had a bearing of authority that Mort couldn't disregard.

"Your father," he began again, and this time all hint of the accent was buried, "had been assisting us with a very important program."

The phrase "limp wrist pencil pusher" flashed across Mort's psyche and he smiled.

"In exchange for his assistance, he had been granted terms for an early release."

"Is that what you call it?" Mort said. "So I assume he wasn't buried on prison grounds, you being a man of your word and all."

"Oh, his death had nothing to do with his involvement with us, I assure you," Dr. Martin replied.

"Uh-huh," Mort said, "what did you give him?"

"His involvement was purely observational—"

"Not the last time," Mort pressed. "What did you give him back in '46 when he was at Folsom?"

Dr. Martin leaned back in his chair.

"Mister LeFrance, I think you need to take our conversation more seriously. You're going to be in prison for a long time. I'd like to offer you the opportunity of reducing your sentence."

"Can you get me let out today?" Mort replied. "We can go have this discussion at a bar. It's been a while since my last Anchor Steam and I always think better when I'm about twelve beers in. I'm a lot more agreeable too. I'll sign just about anything you put in front of me. You might even get lucky."

Dr. Martin laughed in a way that expressed more malice than humor; the sound came out in a putter like the engine of an old-time car.

"It's premature to discuss your release, but I do assure you that if you cooperate, you will be able to enjoy your ... Anchor Steam relatively soon."

"No good."

"Excuse me?"

"No good, it's either today or never."

Dr. Martin removed his spectacles. He rubbed his fingers over his eyes and took a deep breath before returning the thin rim lenses to his face. Though the glasses were fragile enough that Mort could crush them with his palm, the lean biker got another, even stronger, impression of lurking menace. The smoke came to him, whispering secrets directly to his mind. The face before him was a mask, beneath it lurked a beast, something even Mort should fear.

"Mister LeFrance, I am an old man. I've been working in my field for many years and I've had many masters, but my foremost master has always been the truth."

"Are you going anywhere with this?"

The doctor ignored the quip.

"I'm old enough now to have the advantage of hindsight. As I look back, I see many paths I might have taken. I also see the travels of men who took other paths. I see their journeys. I see the hardships they endured, the errors they made, and the results of their choices. It's all clear. But even so, some things remain obscured. I believe you can be a great asset in clearing up some of those mysteries."

"I told you," Mort repeated, "get me out of this monkey suit and we can have a talk."

"What you're saying is quite impossible." Dr. Martin gave a pained smile. "Just consider for a moment the thing you've most wanted your whole life. Consider being close to it, as close as I am to you. Imagine reaching out for it only to have it pulled eternally away. How would you feel? What would you be prepared to do to achieve it?"

"I'd probably go and drown my sorrows in a dozen or so bottles of Anchor Steam. But like I said before, I do my best thinking *after* I've had a drink, not before."

Dr. Martin's jaw clenched. For a moment, the skin stretched taut across his face and he took on the aspect of an animated skull. Mort felt the presence of the smoke around him draw closer.

"Mister LeFrance, for the last time, I would like to politely request that you help me continue the work I began with your father..."

Mort sensed the smoke swell up in the room. He couldn't determine whether it was acting on his volition or its own. The power was invisible to Dr. Martin, but its presence created a dampening effect, drowning out the doctor's words. Mort ceased to hear the doctor speak, and as his concentration focused, he urged the smoke to advance upon doctor.

Tendrils formed into fine points that wiggled through the air to find Dr. Martin's mouth, ears, eyes, and nostrils. With a great breath, Dr. Martin was made to inhale, and Mort glanced around in surprise as all of a sudden the room was vacated of smoke.

The doctor sat at rigid, docile attention.

Mort stared at him.

The doctor stared back.

"You will forget about me," Mort said, speaking on instinct, the words a command.

Dr. Martin nodded.

"You will get up and leave this room never to return."

Another nod.

"We're done here," Mort howled past the doctor to Officer Parks.

As Parks came to the door, Dr. Martin scurried to his feet and made his exit. He virtually slithered away, like a raccoon fearful of headlights as it dug through neighborhood trash. Mort felt sickened as he watched the strange man go.

A few minutes later, Mort was back in his cell.

"My condolences for your loss," Parks said as he removed the cuffs.

"Yeah, it's a shame he went so peacefully, I'm not sure he got what he deserved," Mort said. "Don't worry, Parks, I've got no need to go and pay my respects. I'll be doing the rest of my time as quiet as a kitten."

Parks took a long look at the back of Mort's neck. Then he slipped the cuffs onto his belt and turned to walk away.

CHAPTER 15

Graduation

At the end of their senior year, Mickey and William were looking for something to do. Picking up a paper, Mickey called out a suggestion.

"Let's go check out this new movie, Star Wars."

"Aw," William replied, "space movies are for grade school kids. Shiny fake looking ships made out of tinfoil that they swing around on a fishing line."

"Naw, something tells me this one will be good."

"As good as your grandmother?"

Mickey gave William a look that made him relent, but he grumbled all the way until the opening score. Then he sat with his mouth agape for the full running time. Mickey was impressed too, but for a different reason. Just as when he was at St. Asors, he got the sense that the universe was trying to tell him something. Here was a film that embraced the concept of extrasensory powers. It was soothing to Mickey to see such a thing presented so publicly, and have it treated with such respect and admiration by the general public. Sitting in the darkness watching Star Wars, he felt less a freak.

***

Mickey and William got into cycling to stay out of trouble. They headed out to Stow, a little village far outside of the Boston suburbs. While riding on the winding country roads, Mickey thought of their old track team buddy, Leo. They had nicknamed him Paavo after the famous Finnish distance runner, Paavo Nurmi. Neither Mickey nor William had seen or heard from Paavo after he left school at the end of his freshman year.

Out of nowhere, Mickey thought of him.

"I wonder what ever happened to Paavo?"

William shrugged and kept riding.

A few minutes later, they rode by a café in a small town. William stopped his bike and looked at the café. Mickey said, "What are you doing?"

William pointed at the door as Paavo stepped out of the restaurant. The guys went over and after much laughing and handclapping, shared summaries of their past three years. Paavo had moved to a high school in Connecticut. At that moment, he was on his way with his parents for a visit to Amherst College, which was out in the direction of the boys' ride.

After Paavo and his folks went on their way, Mickey fished a quarter from his pocket and rubbed it between his thumb and forefinger. He thought William might be interested to know his buddy could use the 'force.' Mickey stared at the quarter until he got William's attention, then spoke with a drawn out emphasis on the last word.

"Don't you think that was a bit odd?"

"What?" William replied.

Mickey flashed him a wry look. "You don't think it was odd that we were just talking about Paavo and—'poof'—he appears?"

William shrugged. "It's just one of those things."

Mickey looked at the quarter. He was very tempted to hand it to William and tell his friend to start flipping. How many would he have to get correct before William started to believe? Ten, fifty, a hundred? Mickey knew with certainty that William's thumb would give out before his predictions did.

"What if it isn't 'one of those things?'"

"Mickey. Really. Shut up." William grabbed his bicycle, mounted, and set off, putting an end to the discussion.

Mickey recalled the sight of his notebook fluttering out the window of the family car when his dad was similarly disturbed by Mickey's insistence. He stuffed the quarter back into his pocket, grabbed his bicycle, and hurried to catch up with William.

***

Graduation came. The powers that be decided that an outside ceremony would be a great idea, so there were the 175 seniors, including Mickey, gathered in the football bleachers on a chilly May evening. The stadium lights were already on. Down on the dais, right at the fifty yard line, sat the superintendent, the principal, and assorted faculty notables. In a revered, albeit elitist tradition, the honor students would receive their diplomas first. Mickey had sneaked into the chosen few by dint of his ability to memorize.

He'd been punished so frequently and sent to memory duty so often at St. Asors that by the time he graduated they had to give him at least twelve pages to memorize to keep him busy for any reasonable length of time. He could do that in an hour. The skill made high school easy. Mickey could regurgitate answers word for word.

At first they accused him of cheating, so he recited an entire chapter of Mrs. Nickerby's literature textbook. When they told him he couldn't do that anymore, Mickey paraphrased. His ability went a long way toward getting him accepted at the University of Wisconsin.

Mickey walked across the stage and hustled into the reception line, anxious to hit the road and drink some beer with his buddies. The line of well-wishers was a much smaller group than that awaiting the rest of the graduates. As more students went through, more people lined up to shake hands. Mickey hurried through the line like one of the players at the end of a little kids' basketball game. "Thank you, thank you, thank you..." pressing flesh in a faux formality.

The line ended in the penumbra of the stadium lights, where it was darker. He was about to walk away and out the gate to freedom when he heard a very soft voice.

"Hey, Mickey."

Mickey turned and looked into the eyes of a beautiful young woman. The portrait in his mind heaved off half a decade of dust and spiderwebs and virtually glowed. She was older now, but there could be no mistake: Carlie!

Before Mickey could say anything, she hugged him with surprising strength. He felt the stirrings of adult love. She backed up and held Mickey by both arms.

"I'm so proud of you," she said, and then kissed him full on the lips.

The world slowed and became strange like on the stairwell in William's house. Mickey didn't know what was happening, and he couldn't will his body to obey. He wasn't sure if it was her proximity that paralyzed him or some other power. There was a tingling and a ringing in his ears. He felt as if he had been transported to some other reality.

The sound of whistling and catcalls erupted behind him. Instinct made him turn, and he saw William and his buddies. Then he heard his dad call. "Mickey?" The world closed in.

Suddenly disoriented, Mickey was barely aware of a small hand grabbing his and sliding an envelope into it. Terror clutched at Mickey's heart, for he had a sense that he was about to lose her again. He fought against what felt like a strange sort of gravity, but somehow knew he was about to lose. His focus went to securing the letter, and before anyone could approach, Mickey slid the envelope into the inside pocket of his suit jacket.

The action seemed to release a tidal wave of emotions. Mickey felt dizzy. The third rail sense was buzzing and he didn't know why. What was going on? What was this strange energy pulsating around him? Had *she* caused it? Suddenly, he realized he didn't know who he meant by "she." Had there been somebody there? He squinted his eyes and reached for a memory that wouldn't come to him.

Mickey recognized his dad's features, and William's, and other friends from high school. There was a feeling of acceleration. A flask tilted into Mickey's mouth; William's flask. Mickey felt the burn of something down his throat. The first drink was followed by another and then a third. The graduation celebration ensued, exploding around Mickey and swallowing him whole.

The next day, Mickey awoke bruised and fully clothed with a headache to kill an elephant. When the obstruction to his thinking abated, he finally remembered ... *the letter*! He began patting his pockets in the grip of morning terror.

He found only stale air.

He turned his pockets inside out, stripped his clothing, and then turned out every drawer in his room.

The letter was gone. He was devastated.

Had he imagined it?

Had he imagined her?

Was it all a dream?

He sat and held his head in his hands, overcome by a sense of confusion, sadness and terrible loss. With shaking hands he reached toward his notebook to record yet another incident he couldn't comprehend.

***

Summer passed and the Haddons packed Mickey off to the wild, wild, West—the University of Wisconsin. They sent him with an antique olive-green trunk reinforced with brown canvas straps. It had two clip latches on the front and a padlock-type hasp in the center. It was huge and weighed 130 pounds. Back then, airlines had the funny idea that it was their job to help passengers get to where they needed with their stuff, so off the trunk and Mickey went on a TWA 707, one stop in O'Hare and then directly to Madison.

Mickey ended up in a dorm overlooking Lake Mendota. The old stone buildings, oak-tree lined shore and magnificent waters made him feel like he was in a Jimmy Stewart movie. He opened up the trunk with his belongings and started unpacking and putting away clothes. To his dismay, he saw that his mother had sewn "Mickey Haddon" into all of his underwear. That was going to go over great in the dorm.

He pulled out some pictures of his folks, an old Corona typewriter, and there at the bottom was his Stoneham High yearbook and diploma. His mother must have snuck them in. Mickey had not seen the diploma since graduation night.

He picked it up, and an envelope fell out.

Now Mickey remembered! Rather than let his friends see him with the goods, he had transferred the note from his pocket to the diploma as he walked to the parking lot on graduation night. There it had been all this time! He checked to see that his door was locked, sat down on the bed and held up the envelope. Across the front, in delicate letters, was written a single word: *Mickey*.

He tore it open. The note was written on expensive cloth grade paper. He could once again feel the small, warm fingers that had passed it to him. He read:

Dear Mickey,

I know you have an awareness beyond what others can see. It's what drew me to you in the first place. I don't know if it's a gift or a curse but I do know there are more out there than just you and me. I have to warn you of danger. When I'm near you, an energy is created which I believe can draw out the shadows. I don't know if staying away will keep you safe, but it's the only thing I can think of. Be careful! Trust your instincts. If someone gives off dangerous vibrations, take action! He's going to come again soon. I will find you when the darkness has passed.

— C

Mickey put the letter down. There was no contact information provided.

He carefully folded the letter and put it into his pocket next to his heart. He lay back on his dorm cot, stared at the ceiling for a while, and shut his eyes.

CHAPTER 16

Paperclip

At the end of three years, Carlie was a much different person than the timid girl who had come knocking on Gabby's door with a folded paper under her arm. Gabby had noticed the change. The girl who used to sit before her for their afternoon tea was gone, replaced by a confident and accomplished woman. Gabby was glad, but she couldn't escape a sense of melancholy that, no matter what happened in the future, the relationship they'd enjoyed the last few years would soon come to an end. Gabby was still processing these thoughts when Carlie surprised her with a question.

"Did you ever know two members of Stanford faculty named Alan and Shalla Stillman?"

Gabby's eyes went wide as if she'd been struck by lightning, and then she covered her mouth with her hand. "I've been blind this whole time," she exhaled, "of course, how could I have missed it? You are the mirror image of her. Shalla was your mother, wasn't she?"

Carlie nodded. "Please don't tell anyone."

"Oh, my dear, your secret is safe with me," Gabby replied, "you were wise not to broadcast your identity. Yes, to answer your question; yes, I knew Alan and Shalla." Gabby leaned back in her chair and reflected. "That was a strange time, and not so long ago. Bad decisions were made, and I fear more negative consequences are yet to come as a result."

"Why? What happened?"

"Stanford is a large campus, child, but gossip travels at the speed of light. About the time your parents were here, a lot of money was rolling in; government money. Young men determined to make a name for themselves are always quick to grab the big dollars before questioning the work they'll be asked to do. There was a culture here that seduced a lot of good men into dangerous territory." Gabby thought for a moment, but then she sighed. "That's about the extent of what I know."

"Who might know more?" Carlie pressed.

Gabby laughed. "You're not going to get too many confessions out of the academic types. Those stuffy old crones are so obsessed with their legacy that they've developed black spots in their memory for any missteps they might have taken along the way. If you start asking questions on campus, you'll get nothing but cold shoulders and blank stares at best, and at worst, who knows what they might do ... expulsion for a start? Restraining orders?"

"Just for asking questions?" Carlie was shocked. "I've never been in any trouble and I'm a top student; doesn't that count for anything?"

Gabby shook her head. "I'm sorry but it doesn't, not for matters like this. I know we say academic standing means something, but it just ... doesn't ..."

Carlie stared into her teacup. Through the dark liquid, it was impossible to see the bottom of the cup.

"There was an incident," Gabby said, probing her memory for something that could help, "something happened in L.A. that brought some heat. The government stooges were a presence on campus after that; they were overt for a while despite their best efforts to disguise themselves. People are never as clever as they think." Gabby rolled her eyes back into her head as if probing for a memory. "A young journalism student ... let's see, what was her name? Roberta? Ruth? Ruth something, something unusual. Ruth Nooker! She'd been there, at L.A., she got escorted off campus here. It was a terrible scandal."

"Ruth Nooker," Carlie whispered.

Gabby looked up, and reached forward to grab both of Carlie's hands. She stared at the young woman with grave urgency. "Be very careful, Carlie. There are forces at work here I can't protect you from. You've got a great future ahead of you. It might be best to forget the past and focus on creating a better future for yourself."

"But what if the past comes looking for me?" Carlie replied.

Gabby nodded. "It very well might."

"Then you know why I have to ask those questions."

***

Carlie did let it go, for a while anyway. She was already planning for post-graduation. At the end of the semester the campus had largely cleared out. Carlie was relaxing on a patch of grass when an impulse led her to the Journalism department. She stopped at the office and spoke with the administrative assistant.

"Hello," Carlie said, "I'm doing a research project on successful Stanford alumni. I was wondering if you had any information on Ruth Nooker?"

The administrative assistant was an older woman with a blue beehive hairdo. She peered at Carlie through gaudy wing-tipped spectacles, but at the mention of Ruth, she softened.

"Oh, Ruth, what a wonderful person; it's sad what happened to her."

"Excuse me?"

"Her professors were very proud of her, she was working as a reporter with the *Boston Daily Register*, but then she disappeared. The police never found anything."

Carlie recoiled. "When was this?"

"'69 or '70," the assistant replied. "Her father still lives out in Sausalito; he never got over it."

Carlie thanked the woman and headed straight home to Gabby. She asked if she could borrow the Citroen with the explanation that she had a few free days and a strong desire to drive up the coast. Gabby agreed of course.

***

There was only one Nooker in the Sausalito phone book: Chuck Nooker. He had a roofing business. A phone call to his office revealed that Chuck was out on a job, but he could probably be found at the nearest bar to the job site. Carlie scribbled down the address.

Later that evening, Carlie found herself walking into a dive next to the beach. A utility truck with 'Nooker Roofing' painted on the side indicated she was at the right place. She was worried she wouldn't be able to find him, but fortunately the bar had only one patron. Carlie bought a couple beers and brought them over to the table. Chuck looked up, smiled skeptically, then turned back to the half-finished beer already sitting in front of him.

"Sorry, I'm not interested."

"Excuse me?"

"Pretty girls don't come up to guys like me in bars and offer them beers for nothing. I'm guessing that whatever you want is something I don't need."

Carlie set the beers on the table. She thought for a moment, but quickly decided a bold approach was the best.

"My name is Carlie Tillford," she stated. "My parents died in 1970."

"Sorry for your loss," Chuck said, not looking up.

"We lived north of Boston."

Chuck said nothing, but he tensed.

"They never found the guy. I gave a description to the police, but they never even looked."

Chuck turned to look at her, the hint of emotion around his eyes. "Why are you telling me this?"

"Because your daughter disappeared three weeks before this happened. I think the same person might have been responsible."

Chuck's hands tightened around his beer. He lifted the bottle to his lips and took a long, slow drink that finished the bottle. When he was done, he put the empty back on the table and reached for one of the two that Carlie had brought.

"The last time I talked to Ruth," Chuck said, his voice cracking at the mention of his daughter's name, "she told me she had discovered something big. She said that if anything happened to her, she gave me something to tell the authorities. She's been gone for five years and you know what? You're the first person who has come to ask. You'd think there would be more of an investigation, wouldn't you? It's almost as if somebody's pumping the brakes."

"What did she tell you?"

"Honestly, it don't make any sense to me." He drained another beer. "Paperclip. That was the word. She said to tell them to look into paperclip."

"Paperclip," Carlie replied. She couldn't decide if she'd gotten closer to resolving the mystery or drifted farther way.

***

Carlie's head was filled with thoughts as she began her drive from Sausalito back to Stanford. As she looked out the window, she noted the roofs of the houses; little rectangles speckled in and out of the hillsides.

"Like letters in an alphabet nobody can read," she muttered.

A chill went down her spine. The danger felt suddenly close.

Passing a movie theater, she saw a sign on the marquee: 'Coming Soon: Star Wars!'

The words set Carlie to thinking and she was still deep in thought when she pulled into Gabby's home and returned the keys.

"I'm going to Boston for a couple days," she said.

"Oh," Gabby replied, surprised. "What for?"

"I have some things to look into." She thought for a moment before adding, "And a message to deliver."

CHAPTER 17

Cyclops

Mort walked out of prison in the fall of 1980 and set his focus on finding a new dog. He was uncomfortable in the Gary, Indiana/Chicago megapolis, so with the small allowance they doled out when he was released, he bought a ticket on a Greyhound down to south central Indiana.

He slept most of the way, head against the cold window, watching the land pass by. Every now and then he caught a glimpse of black smoke stretching off into the distance.

At a stop in West Lafayette, Mort decided he couldn't stand another second on the bus. He stood up and made his way off.

"We're leaving in ten minutes," the driver said.

Mort raised his hand without making eye contact with the man. He sauntered away and didn't come back.

First things first. He needed a grubstake.

There were always liquor stores near the bus stops. There were limits to the cruelty of the universe. After crawling out of a stinky silver liner people couldn't be expected to walk an extra block for a drink. Mort didn't have a weapon besides his natural nastiness and intimidating physique. They'd be sufficient. He glanced around and soon enough, a tendril coalesced to direct him. He sauntered over to a dingy-looking place across the highway.

He pushed open the glass door, which rang a bell. The man at the register noticed him and looked up from the paper he was reading. He was a middle-aged, balding man with a short-sleeve button up shirt. He wasn't offensive-looking, but he couldn't exactly be called 'clean' either.

"Can I help you, sir?"

Mort strolled over to the counter, scanning left and right as he made his way. When he arrived, he put his hands on the man's paper and fixed him with a deadly glare.

"All the cash, now." The words came out in a bestial growl.

The man complied. He opened the register and put the bills on the counter.

Mort had just begun sliding them into his hand when he felt the coldness of a double-barreled Remington shotgun pressed up against the back of his neck.

"Hands up, cowboy!"

Mort put up his hands. But he was not going to jail again. He jerked his head one way and his arms another, swinging around with a fierce backhand that knocked the barrel sideways. There was a deafening blast and the man behind the counter was blown backward five feet as the two double ought magnum slugs tore through his chest.

At the sight of where the shot had gone, the assistant collapsed to his hands and knees and threw up. He was out of the fight.

Mort turned back to the counter and resumed stacking the cash, which he stuffed into his pocket.

"Look what you did!" the assistant cried. "Are you satisfied?"

"It weren't my finger on the trigger, and to answer your question, no, I'm not," Mort replied. He opened his hands. "Keys!"

The assistant recovered enough to try to strike Mort with the shotgun. Mort caught the barrel in one hand then grabbed the man by the throat with his other. Mort stared into his assailant's eyes and caught a vision of the man selling drugs to kids near a local school. Mort sneered, lifted the assistant into the air and then smashed him back down upon the glass counter top, crushing it into shards.

"Keys!"

Bleeding and in agony, the man produced a set of car keys from his pocket.

"It's a gray van," he said.

"I know." Mort took the shotgun in both hands and slammed the butt into the injured man's face. He went limp. Mort struck two more times anyway, then used the man's shirt to clean the blood from the stock.

He locked the front door and switched the sign to 'closed' before pulling both bodies out of sight. He started reaching for a bottle of Wild Turkey, then caught himself and went top shelf instead. He pulled the cork of something fancy, took a long draw, and scowled. He threw the bottle down to shatter on the floor and reached again for the Wild Turkey.

Mort felt pretty good as he stepped outside. He failed to notice the security cameras that had recorded the whole scene.

A few days later, the Indiana police matched his face to their criminal files and came up with the name Mortimer LeFrance, but by then, Mort had already headed south.

***

Mort found a job roofing. The guys in prison had told him it was good ex-con work. There were plenty of contractors looking for cheap labor; no questions asked, no federal income tax filed, and payment in cash. He was strong and he made a fair amount of money. Enough money to look for a dog.

The dog-fighting scene dominated the underworld entertainment of rural southern Indiana. He became a regular at a notorious pit in the backwoods outside of French Lick. The inhumane savagery of the sport appealed to him. He became fascinated with a Shepherd/Rottweiler cross named Cyclops.

Cyclops was an aging veteran, never beaten although the physical feature that gave him his name bore witness to a close call with an over-sized pitbull. Mort saw the dog fight five times before he decided that Cyclops was the dog he had to have.

"I do hope that puppy's for sale," he said, approaching the handler.

"Everything's for sale," the handler replied.

Mort gave a number.

The beefy owner scratched the sun-burned back of his neck where three rolls of hard fat intersected a dirty T-shirt, which was chafing. He finished the itching, tucked his thumbs under the suspenders of his loose blue jean overalls, changed his tune, and said the dog was too valuable to part with.

Mort came back a week later. As he entered the big tent, he noticed the owner scanning the folding chairs as if looking for someone. When he saw Mort, he beckoned him over. When Mort approached, he grabbed Mort's bicep and pulled him so close that Mort could smell pickled eggs, beer and cigarettes on his breath. The owner looked around and then muttered *sotto voce*, "You still want Cyclops?"

"Sure I want him. What's the deal?"

"He's the best fightin' dog I ever had but he's too damn mean. He bites anyone who gets near him. Last week, he put a twenty-five stitch wound in the old lady's calf. I told her to stay away from that damn dog. Now it's my fault and I gotta get rid of him. I ain't givin' him away, though. Three hundred dollars and he's your'n. Only reason I'm asking you is cuz you look like you can handle him."

"I'll give you one fifty."

The handler shook his head and released his grip. It was time for Mort to apply his own. He drove his thumb into the pit of the man's elbow.

"One fifty," Mort said again. "You're in a jam, it's a fair deal."

The handler had been around enough mad dogs to recognize one. He nodded.

A veneer of calm returned to Mort's features. He pulled out the wallet hooked to his belt by a trucker's chain and peeled off the cash. He had thirty-four bucks left over.

The handler led him outside to a rusted out pickup truck with several large boxes. One of the boxes was shaking. He reached into a plastic ice cooler and grabbed a putrid piece of meat, unlatched the box and threw the meat toward the back. Then, with surprising quickness for one so large, he reached in with a leash, snapped onto the collar and pulled out Cyclops. Cyclops came because his collar was a steel choke chain with sharp two-inch teeth. The handler gave the leash to Mort and said, "Good luck, boy."

Mort wasn't sure if the quip was directed at him or the dog.

Cyclops sniffed Mort and then lay down with his head on Mort's shoe.

"I'll be," said the handler as Mort headed off to his van with Cyclops trotting at a perfect heel.

CHAPTER 18

An Incident on Lake Mendota

Mickey spent his years at Madison drifting through an assortment of liberal arts courses, and as the summer of '81 approached he was close to graduating with a degree in Psychology. Like most young men, he was uncertain about the future even with his gift of perception. As the years passed, he had become more adept at quelling his insights. When he felt an impulse to turn left, he went right and didn't look back. In time, the calling became less insistent, but there were still moments when the power manifested as an involuntary response. As always, he kept careful records in his Big Chief tablet, there was something about the act of writing that seemed to make the feelings go away.

Mickey kept Carlie's letter on him always. He didn't read it often, but he found comfort in the heft and physicality of it. The letter served as a reminder that he was not alone. It gave him the strength he needed to carry on.

Sometimes, walking through campus, he'd catch a glimpse of a woman with a familiar figure and his breath would catch in his throat. But then she'd turn and he'd start breathing again.

It was the eyes.

Of all things, Mickey was certain that if he lived to be a hundred he'd still be able to recognize her from her eyes. No other girl had the same combination of peace and intensity as Carlie.

At the end of May, he stood in Camp Randall with thousands of other graduates and was pronounced a Bachelor of Arts. His next occupation was a big question mark. He knew little beyond the fact that he had three months of summer lifeguarding guaranteed.

He considered signing up for TeachUSA; an organization in the market for warm bodies willing to go to troubled schools. In return, survivors were promised two years of sink or swim teaching experience, a small stipend, free tuition for a masters' degree and a teaching certificate at the end of the road. The schools were, on the whole, located in poor areas, often tortured by an atmosphere of violence and hopelessness. It looked good to Mickey compared to bartending when the lifeguard docks closed, so he applied and was accepted.

He had a plan: Enjoy the summer.

The lazy days spent working on a student dock on Lake Mendota passed soporifically. August rolled around and Mickey took a week off to visit his parents in Massachusetts. When he returned, he spotted a new girl on the dock; a lissome brunette, no bigger than half a minute, with touches of auburn in her hair, an adorable figure and features hidden by over-sized sunglasses. There was an energy about her that Mickey couldn't ignore.

"Who is she?" he asked Ron.

His fellow lifeguard was a go-lucky fraternity type who never felt quite right with his shirt on. Ron was one of those Scandinavians with a shock of hair so white, it appeared bleached. He had a ruddy red face to go with it and an all-world attitude. Too much time in the sun and too many nights on State Street had taken its toll on Ron's eloquence.

"I don't know but she's hot, and she's turning into a regular, which is good for us, eh?"

Ron made an hourglass shape with his hands.

Mickey thought he might get something more useful out of Paul. Paul was a philosophy major who spent all his free time meditating by the lake. There was entirely too much useless education wasting away at the University beach.

Paul sighed. "As usual, Ron makes no sense. You would not say she is hot any more than you would say the Rocky Mountains are hot. Like an unapproachable snow-covered summit, she is both unbearably attractive and deeply intimidating all at once: a force of nature; breathtaking and beckoning, but unattainable."

"Yeah! And older!" Ron interrupted. "A law student or something. Too bad she's so cold. But she is hot." Ron's discourse was interrupted by the arrival of Nuavel Grant. Nuavel was a physical specimen, and just now he was carrying a six pack under his arm. Mickey shook his head, expecting the kind of trouble he didn't want or need.

Nuavel played for the Badgers. He had recently been named a preseason Second Team All-American at defensive back. He was a consensus First Team All-American asshole and a constant pain to all the guards. Nuavel swore, he talked big, he annoyed the women and he was mean, quick to anger, and always looking for trouble.

"Uh-oh, looks like Nuavel caught word of the sale at Roundy's," Ron said.

"What sale?" Mickey replied.

"Roundy's just got a truckload in; they've been selling them for ninety-nine cents a six pack."

"No kidding?" Mickey responded. "I guess I'm heading to Roundy's after this."

From the surly look on Nuavel's face, the guards guessed he had already finished off about half his beers. Their suspicions were confirmed when Nuavel began chucking empties at ducks. He had a great arm. Some of the bottles landed in the water, where they bobbed. Others shattered, leaving shards of glass all over the beach.

"Hey, Nuavel," Ron hollered.

Nuavel turned with an aggressive scowl on his face.

"Did you know lifeguards are cops?"

Nuavel stood for a moment, the bottle cocked and ready to throw. He stared at Ron and Ron stared back, not in the least perturbed by the fact that lifeguards were not cops. After a few tense seconds, Nuavel turned away without acknowledging Ron, but he dropped his arm and slipped the bottle back into its cardboard carrier.

They waited for Nuavel to get out of earshot and started to laugh.

"Well, you sure stood up to Nuavel," Mickey said, "but that little brunette shut you down?"

Ron rolled his eyes. "Yeah, like I said, she's a cold one."

'Cold' was Ron's description for any girl who did not jump at the chance to go to bed with him. Having been subjected to Ron's obnoxious overtures, many girls would never return to the beach. But as he had just shown, Ron had a way about him as well. Any woman who could rebuff Ron was more than a little intriguing. Mickey's interest was piqued.

***

Mickey was stationed on a pier next to one of the summer student dorms when he received an insight into the transcendent paranormal power binding those who see beyond the gates of reality. It had been a perfect sunbathing day when Ron's paragon of beauty showed up. As always, a pair of gigantic sunglasses covered the majority of her face. The guards sat high up in their chairs and pretended not to be affected, but even from a distance Mickey felt a warmth as she walked by.

She spread out a beach towel at the edge of the metal dock. She wore a white bikini top with an aqua towel chastely wrapped around her waist. Sometimes, in addition to knowing what was going to happen, Mickey knew what was happening in the present when no one else did, and on this instance, he chose not to ignore his insight. Just then it confided that she wore nothing beneath her towel.

The girl asked the coed next to her to untie her bikini strap. Her friend began to rub suntan lotion between her freckled shoulder blades. Mickey was still recovering from St. Asors. The nuns admonished the boys to pray when tempted by impure thoughts.

Mickey was halfway through his fifth Act of Contrition when Nuavel Grant showed up again on the pier, accompanied by some kind of a German Shepherd monster dog that went at least 150 pounds. Mickey suspected the beer incident from the other day had stuck in Nuavel's craw, which was why he'd decided to return toting an illegal attack dog.

The beast would have scared Godzilla. It had more muscles than Nuavel, and probably more brains. Nuavel pretended to ignore the creature that loyally trotted alongside him.

Anyone who'd ever been traumatized by a dog was sure to be triggered by Nuavel's beast.

Like the new girl.

Who knew?

As Nuavel arrived, Mickey put up his hand in a futile attempt to get his attention, but Nuavel and everyone else ignored the signal because of a scream, followed by the collective breath intake of every guy on the dock.

As soon as the young brunette spied the dog, she jumped up and hollered. Her top fell off and, more sensationally, so did her towel.

Mickey was right.

Nothing on.

This spectacular full Monty did not last because she jumped in the water. The screaming continued. As Ron tried to reason with Nuavel and the dog, Mickey went over to the edge to help. His reality began to tingle and he couldn't tell if it was caused by the ensuing chaos or something more.

Mickey was hoping for assistance, but the discussion behind him had gotten loud and angry. Then Mickey heard a piercing song-like whistle. He was subconsciously aware of the sound and would think about it later, but at the time the melody was blurred in with the other events. His consciousness was dominated by the protestations of Nuavel, who was yelling in a voice three octaves below middle C.

"It's. Not. My. Dog. Man!"

Nuavel and Ron were completely occupied in chest bumping and man-dance threats, and the girl continued to scream. So Mickey went for it. It was not a difficult save. There she was, splashing and screaming and treading water. He reached in, grabbed her around the forearm and pulled. Up she came, waist high, revealing a petite but perfect pair of breasts.

It was the touch that did it.

The tingle of psychic energy coalesced into insight.

This was Carlie! He'd found her!

The revelation made Mickey pause, and he froze with a stupefied look on his face.

In the midst of the chaos, Carlie's screams changed pitch and brought Mickey back to the present. Her frightened howling became angry.

"Let me go!" she hollered.

Mickey looked around for advice. Ron and Nuavel had drawn a crowd. No one noticed a strange man up on the shore under the big trees, walking toward the dock. A day at the beach was turning into a Smothers Brothers skit. The man on shore was limping. Mickey thought perhaps the man would help, until he got a better look and did a double take as a shiver went through him.

The stranger was wearing a ten gallon hat. Under the hat, long flowing hair hung freely across his shoulder blades. He was staring at Mickey. Their eyes locked and there was an intense and inexplicable shared recognition. Something about Mickey surprised the cowboy. He turned and hobbled away. The girl in the lake began talking, but Mickey couldn't make out the words.

Mickey released her. She fell.

Splash!

She went under, came up, and choked out, "You idiot!"

"Are you OK?" Mickey asked.

"Stop looking!" she yelled, and began to cry.

A siren pierced the afternoon air. Someone had run into the dorms and called rescue. Either Nuavel had a heart or figured this event might lead to an interview with the police. Whatever his motivation, he turned and hustled away. The big dog was still barking its head off at the helpless female until another shrill whistle pierced the afternoon madness.

It was the cowboy.

The giant dog backed off from the edge, peed on the lifeguard stand, and almost as an afterthought picked up Mickey's prized Bucky Badger sweatshirt that was piled in a heap by the guard's chair. The dog trotted off after the stranger in the shadows, who was limping away at a respectable pace. Nuavel observed the dog's retreat, turned to Ron, and said, "See?" and strutted off. After a few steps, he stopped, turned and gave everyone the finger, then turned again and skipped away.

Someone grabbed Mickey's bicep and said, "Get away, will you! Back off and turn around. All of you!"

It was a friend of the dunk tank victim. The guards retreated to give her some privacy. There was some sobbing and dripping water and then the dock shook slightly as someone climbed up the ladder. When Mickey and Ron turned back, the small woman had a bigger towel wrapped around her entire torso. Her eyes met Mickey's. He felt that third rail shock he remembered from the time Wayne asked to borrow Curly's suit. She flinched too. A stray pencil rolled across the dock between them in a way that struck Mickey as unnatural.

Had she felt that?

"I'm sorry ... I heard you scream and I tried to help you," he said.

Carlie nodded. A vortex of energy surrounded them. It was uncomfortable and chaotic.

Carlie looked as if she was about to say something, but then the police arrived. Mickey was hustled off to a quiet area and try as he might, he couldn't escape the officers until he'd given a statement. By the time he'd finished, the girl and her friend had gone and a state of normalcy had returned.

Mickey couldn't decide whether he'd won or lost.

CHAPTER 19

Hop In

Several months of roofing work had helped Mort get through the transition to freedom, but summer had come and he suddenly felt a need for travel. It felt right to have Cyclops beside him in the van, and the open road called with more urgency than he'd known in a long time. Mort had traded vans three times since the one he had acquired at the Indiana liquor store. Still, it never hurt to put an extra barricade in between himself and the authorities. Mort slipped into the driver's seat, put the vehicle in gear and drove out to a rest stop beside the interstate. He pulled off the plates and waited for a vehicle with no passengers to arrive.

An elderly man in a flannel shirt pulled up and slammed his door, on the way to the bathroom. Mort was behind the vehicle swapping out plates before the new arrival had even entered the facility.

The whole ordeal was routine. Mort changed his plates frequently. When he returned to his car, the lean biker was pleased to see Cyclops scanning the area for threats.

Mort scratched the animal behind the ear, jumped back into his van and drove to the first exit.

At the top of the ramp, Mort gripped the wheel and closed his eyes. He took a deep breath and when he opened them, the black smoke trailed off into the distance to the left, crossing the bridge that spanned the interstate.

Mort went left and drove for a long time in silence, allowing the hum of the road and the panting of Cyclops to soothe him into a meditative state. When he needed to sleep he'd stop at public rest areas and catch an hour or so of shut eye.

Mort was coming back onto the highway after a nap outside of Champaign, Illinois when he saw something that grabbed his attention. A hitchhiker stood on the on-ramp, wearing platform shoes, paisley bell bottoms and a denim work shirt. He had on John Lennon glasses and wore a ponytail halfway down his back. He was trying to grow a mustache, but the kid couldn't have been more than twenty and that wasn't working out so well for him. At first, Mort considered blowing by, but then he remembered his easy score from the last time he'd picked somebody up. He slowed the van to a halt.

"Hi, I'm Quicksilver," the kid said.

"Where you headed?"

"Madison. I go to school there."

Mort gestured for the kid to climb in. The vehicle accelerated down the ramp.

"Where the hell's Madison?" Mort asked.

"Really?"

Mort gave the kid the kind of look that made him straighten up and answer, "Well, actually, you're headed there, sir. Rockford's about three hours away and then the state line and you're almost there."

Gazing through the windshield, Mort perceived no objection from the smoke. He settled back and drove in absolute silence.

On the outskirts of Rockford, Mort looked at the gauge and said, "I might be taking you to Madison but you know what, son? I'm plumb out of gas. Can you help out?"

In the back, Cyclops snarled.

Quicksilver swallowed hard. "I got ten dollars but I need some of it."

Mort pulled into a Texaco station. "Give me the ten," he said, in a tone that didn't invite contradiction.

"Um, sure." Quicksilver fished out the money. "You know, sir, I think I'll get out now."

Mort didn't look up at this, but he smiled.

"No," he said, drawing out the 'o' into almost a falsetto. "You ain't gettin' out. We're having a fine conversation. Don't go and ruin it by bein' rude."

Cyclops barked. The kid sat back. Mort filled up the tank and they drove off in silence until shortly after crossing the state line.

"This is turning into a long trip; you're going to have to find a way to pay me a little more."

"You took all I have."

"Now, you and I both know that's not true. You said you go to school in Madison. A fancy college boy like you has to have some money. Hey, Quicksilver. No crying," Mort said, noticing a tear rolling down the kid's cheek.

"Listen, mister. I don't have anything else!"

Mort's jaw hardened. Quicksilver hadn't been so sheltered that he didn't know what was coming.

"Wait, I do have this," the kid said. He opened up his pack and took out tin cylinder that said 'Mr. Chips' along the side.

"Why the hell would I want potato chips?"

"Because it's not potato chips. It's grass. The best. Mendocino Copper. But you have to have connections to sell it. I have a friend who'll give me four hundred dollars for this. Take me to Madison, I'll make the deal, split it with you and you let me go, OK?"

All sorts of possibilities ran through Mort's mind. He nodded.

Two hours later, they pulled into Madison and headed downtown to Mifflin Street—Madison's answer to Haight-Ashbury. The kid directed Mort to a three-story ramshackle house. Mort was considering how to ditch the kid and make off with the cash when he pulled up to the curb. A riotous party was happening on the house's front porch. Several empty half barrels lay in the front yard, a couple of naked coeds were lounging in a kiddie pool, and Led Zeppelin blasted from a set of speakers with homemade eighteen inch woofers. Cyclops began to howl. The minute the van pulled up, a bearded giant smoking a joint stood up and yelled, "Yo, Quicksilver's here and I'll bet he's got some goodies."

Before Mort could react, the mob charged the van. People were reaching in with tens and twenties. Quicksilver looked at Mort helplessly and then started doling out baggies through the window. Nobody paid attention to Mort, so he unsheathed his knife and surreptitiously pressed it into Quicksilver's side.

Quicksilver caught on quickly and passed over the bills. Soon, the people crowding the van were handing their cash directly to Mort. It all made sense to the Mifflin Street partyers.

Suddenly there was the whoop of a police siren and flashing red and blue lights erupted in the mirrors of the van. Everyone froze, including Mort. Everyone that is, except Quicksilver. In a moment that was half blind inspiration and half panic, Quicksilver grabbed at the door handle and slipped out of the van. The mass of people closed the door behind him. Mort noticed the kid slip out with indifference, he gunned the van and headed down the street as a police car got gummed up in the mass of stoned undergrads behind him. Mort felt his pocket bulging with crumpled 10s and 20s.

"Good afternoon's work, eh Cyclops?"

Cyclops yawned.

***

A few minutes later, Mort was well away from the scene and parked by what appeared to be a college dorm on the side of a huge, beautiful lake. He decided to take Cyclops for a walk and regroup. As he got out of the van, he felt a psychic tingle that had not bothered him since his rampage in Boston.

He saw a dock, a lifeguard stand and people sunbathing. He opened the door to leash Cyclops, but the beast jumped out before he could react and headed toward the dock. The big dog fell in beside a huge football player and trotted alongside him on to the pier. There were screams. Mort limped after the dog.

That's when he saw her: Carlie Stillman!

So that's why the smoke had brought him here! But there was something more, some other source of energy that caused a tingle of power to erupt all around him. Mort's eyes narrowed and he scanned the beach as the smoke directed his vision to a lifeguard standing next to Carlie. The tingle Mort felt in the back of his mind indicated an extrasensory connection. Just as Mort felt it, the kid seemed to feel it too and he turned to look at Mort with a quizzical expression. A new player in the game? Mort's muscled tensed and he was just about to act when chaos ensued. Cyclops barked, the girl screamed and the cops where there before Mort could believe it.

"Is this town all cops!" he snarled before whistling at Cyclops to retreat and regroup.

Mort's hands were shaking from what he had seen as he loaded Cyclops back into the van and drove away to find a dark, quiet place where he could think.

He parked in a narrow alley beside an abandoned warehouse and turned off the motor.

It was quiet outside, no sounds of sirens or even traffic to disturb him.

He gripped the steering wheel tightly until the veins bulged on the backs of his hands, then he released his grip and rubbed his eyes with his fingers.

Cyclops began to whimper.

Mort opened his eyes and for a moment he wondered if he'd gone blind.

Then he realized: the smoke had come.

He'd never seen it like this before. It was as if the sun had been extinguished. The smoke ebbed and flowed before him like the rolling of the tide. Mort was paralyzed, his breath caught short in his throat.

"Sissy," he whispered.

At the sound of his mother's name, the smoke began to withdraw. Mort watched with fascination as the darkness retreated into the shadows cast by buildings, garbage cans, and the holes of broken windows. In a minute, he stared at nothing more than a common industrial alley.

"Sissy," he repeated.

The third rail shock he had received from the boy and the girl at the lake resonated inside his skull.

How could he be in the wrong here? His mother had been slain.

His mother!

Images flashed before Mort's eyes, both the scenes he knew and information he hadn't been aware of before.

Alan and Shalla Stillman.

The Stanford experiments.

Ruth Nooker.

Carlie Stillman!

The reporter and the researchers had paid what they owed, but the child remained. He found he had memories of her now. New memories since his encounter at the beach.

He saw pictures of her studying, taking tests, discussing complex points in college classrooms. She was an accelerated student, driven to achieve, and at only 23 she had nearly completed her post-graduate studies.

The girl was a lawyer!

But there was more than that. She spent time in the library looking at archived newspapers.

What was she looking for?

Mort concentrated and he felt the smoke well up around him again.

Him!

That was the answer. The girl was looking for *him*!

Mort let out his breath.

His focus went to the strange lifeguard, the kid with the Twilight Zone eyes. The presence of the kid had pierced his outer defenses. He could feel a strange energy encroaching on his private, internal places and it took a great psychic effort to repel the assault. What new power was this? Mort felt his hands begin to shake again, but then his anger came and pushed the uncertainty away.

He started up his van and headed out of town to a county park fifteen miles away. With distance, the pressure seemed to ease. Mort threw the vehicle in park and tried to make sense of what he'd just experienced. Did proximity to others with the sight augment his abilities? What were the ramifications? Mort crawled into the back of the van and pinched the bridge of his nose with his thumb and forefinger. He couldn't go into battle without knowing the full consequence of these new variables.

Who was that kid?

Before he could explore the question further, exhaustion overtook him. He closed his eyes and the darkness rolled in speaking secrets to his subconscious in a voice that sounded like the whispers of his mother. Mort slept like the dead.

CHAPTER 20

The Swim

The arrival of the cops cleared the beach out, but Mickey was still on duty. He was in a daze about having seen Carlie. Every part of him wanted to leave the beach and scour the city for her, but at the same time he recognized that she knew where to find him. He stayed on duty, though he felt numb.

Ron left at four o'clock, leaving Mickey to work the pier alone until close at eight. Things had settled back into the lazy humdrum of a summer afternoon on the lake when the wind came up. Despite the sun and clear skies, August sometimes brought a breezy chill to the lake. Whitecaps began to appear off Picnic Point. The last sunbathers pulled on sweatshirts as small clouds blew in, but nobody moved to leave because the pier was not about swimming, or even sunbathing. It was about reading, hanging out, listing to WIBA's new FM programming of rock, and finding romance, passion and love—or any combination of the three.

A bright red ball cap with a white W emblazoned on the front blew into the water, and the few remaining nappers woke up as small raindrops began to plink on the steel deck. Students scrambled to grab books, blankets, portable radios and suntan lotion. In an instant, the breeze turned into a sideways hurricane. Then came the deluge.

Stampede!

Mickey checked the lifeboat's mooring and followed the crowd racing up the shore, through the oaks and into the lounge of the nearest lake shore dorm. More clouds moved in and obliterated the last specks of blue sky. Someone turned on a light in the lounge. It seemed like dusk had fallen in an instant.

A crack of lightning followed by an explosive thunderclap signaled the end of the day at the beach, but the rain was too heavy for anyone to leave the temporary shelter of the dorm. Then, as suddenly as it had moved in, the storm abated. The sun peeked out and created a rainbow over Waunakee, the city on the northern shore. Mickey stepped out and gazed up at the high puffy clouds being blown across a crystalline blue sky by a strong north wind.

Familiar with the vagaries of the weather on the lake, Mickey had a pair of sweatpants, an extra sweater, a stocking cap and wool socks to wear with his flip flops stashed away in the gear locker. As everyone else headed off to the library, or supper, or the bars on State Street, Mickey went back out to the lake and climbed up into his chair to sit and reflect on the joy of seeing Carlie and the instinctive terror provoked by the lean man in the cowboy hat.

No sooner had he settled in than a vibration on the chair disrupted Mickey's thoughts, alerting him that someone had come to join him. He turned and was startled to see Carlie emerge onto the platform, carrying an orange thermos. Mickey's heart rate surged, but he didn't move or cry out. He felt like a hiker in the woods who had stumbled upon a deer and feared any kind of noise or action that might scare the beautiful creature away.

She had changed into a modest two-piece tropical swimsuit with a black skirt bottom. The hint of shapely thighs beneath the skirt was somehow more exciting than the stark beauty exposed by the tiny bikini she had worn earlier. The sun was going down, touching off an alpenglow explosion of soft pink light above the tree line of Picnic Point, a half mile across the bay.

She walked directly up to the surprised lifeguard, and touched his arm.

"Hello Mickey," she said. "Don't say anything. I was hoping to have a drink and watch the sunset. Is that OK?"

She took out a Dixie cup and held it under the little white push button spout. She handed the cup to Mickey and, after serving herself, raised the six ounce paper cup against Mickey's in a mock toast.

"To my lifeguard."

Mickey began to protest, but she put two fingers on his lips and whispered, "Shh. Drink."

He sipped and gagged.

"Are you OK?" she asked.

"I'm fine, just a cough. What is this?"

She laughed. "You need much more education. This is a martini."

Mickey felt destabilized. He had a dozen questions to ask her, but just like the days when she was his tutor, he couldn't seem to make his mouth work. The RCA portable radio was playing softly as the sun set across the bay over the Picnic Point treetops. Carlie began to sway in time to Tommy James and the Shondells' *Crystal Blue Persuasion*.

After a moment, she stopped and looked at him.

"I'm a good swimmer," she said. "You probably couldn't tell with that dog scaring me." She turned her face away from Mickey. "Something very bad with a dog happened to me when I was little. I felt a long ago terror today, but it seems to be gone now."

"A terror. . . like whatever caused you to leave St. Asors?"

She started to answer, then tossed back the remainder of her Dixie cup. She put the cup down, and smiled. "Race you to Picnic Point!"

She dove into the water.

It was over a half mile to Picnic Point. Mickey could not very well deprive her of more lifeguarding, so he flipped the sign on the lifeguard chair to 'CLOSED' and dove in after her.

She was a good swimmer, but he was used to swimming a mile every morning before work as part of his lifeguard regimen. He caught up to her in a hundred yards. She refused to slow or even acknowledge his presence. He swam off to her left, so that on every breath he could catch a glimpse of her slight but strong shoulders. Matching his stroke to hers, they soon completed the crossing and swam toward a small run-down fisherman's pier jutting out from the wooded shoreline of the darkening peninsula.

It's good to be young and strong. They swam up and simultaneously, as if rehearsed, put palms face down on the old deck boards, kicked once, and levered themselves up with a half twist. They ended up sitting side-by-side, legs touching, feet dangling in the water. Mickey was on her right. He wrapped an arm around her shoulders. She exhaled and he reached across and put his right hand high up on her thigh.

She startled him. "Don't."

Mortified, he backed off and slid away from her, wondering how to recover. Then she laughed, reached out, and took his hand.

"I mean, don't do it that way. You were very kind to me today. You tried to help. You didn't laugh, and you said you were sorry when you didn't have to. It touched me." She paused. "I was surprised to see you, I'm not used to that; normally I know what's going to happen. The danger is still out there, though."

"The danger you mentioned in your letter?"

Carlie nodded.

"Can you tell me more?"

She shook her head. "I don't understand it fully yet, but I think our combined presence draws him. I should go."

Carlie made to move, but Mickey grasped her arm. "No, not yet."

Carlie looked back, and when their eyes met there was a ripple that pierced him to his core.

"I know you," she said haltingly, "and I know I'm going to be with you for a long time, even though I am leaving Madison in two days. I'm going to be kind to us tonight in a way we will both remember." She took his hand. "Do you know who Lucretius is?"

Mickey thought he did. "You mean that guy with the Jimi Hendrix T-shirt who hangs out with Nuavel?"

She shook her head. "First martinis, now Epicurean philosophy. You need help. Lucretius advised 'a gentle pleasure to soothe the sting.'"

Mickey didn't say anything, and it was the best decision of his life. She leaned into him and they embraced and made both the past and future resonate with electric shock. The heat became too much for Mickey to handle. Partly for comic relief and partly to refrigerate, he pretended to faint and rolled off the dock.

Carlie laughed and followed him in. She put him in a lifesaving cross-chest carry and began hauling him across the lake. For twenty-five yards, Mickey enjoyed the softness of her touch and went with the flow. Then he escaped and began to swim slowly toward the far-off shore. She swam beside him in the moonlight's reflection; a long shimmering path of light all the way across to the pier.

But the night's surprises were not over. The silence was broken by the faint sounds of a motor, which grew louder as a small light appeared in the distance. The motor got louder and the light got bigger. Soon, they could see a slowing boat and a searchlight scanning the water.

"It's our patrol boat!"

Voices carry over the stillness of a lake. Someone must have heard and called the cops. If Mickey was just a run of the mill drunken student, it would not be a big deal to break the rules. They'd probably just haul them to shore, take names and give out warnings. But he was a guard, the one who was supposed to be keeping the lake free of night swimmers. He'd get fired.

"Carlie. You have got to stay out of sight. Go under every time the light comes by."

A searchlight sweep stayed in one spot for only five or ten seconds. No problem staying under for that. Unfortunately, the patrol boat's random search course was zeroed in on their location.

The boat was going to hit them!

Mickey thought about yelling and giving up, but things were happening too fast. He took a chance that the motor would drown out his voice and yelled, "Go deep, stay under as long as you can." As she dove, he risked an extra second to stare at her beautiful legs arching up in pike position as she submerged.

He followed.

It was too dark to gauge depth, so he swam as deep as he could and then leveled out in the direction the boat had come from. His lungs began to ache. He felt like his head was starting to pop from the inside out. Then there was the sound of a propeller above, but he could not tell if it was coming or going. He resolved to count to fifteen and then come up. When he did, he exploded at the surface, gasping, and looked around.

No Carlie.

Then, beside him, a second explosion and his lovely mermaid was spitting a stream of water in his face and laughing. The patrol boat was down at the far end of the bay. They got busy swimming and in a matter of minutes were pulling ashore on the now dark dock.

They walked up the shore together through shadowy silhouettes of the towering oaks that line Lake Mendota. They approached the grad student dorms where she was staying.

"Thank you," Mickey said.

She stopped. "I've changed my mind."

She threw her beach towel down on the grass and sat primly in the moonlight. "Do what you want."

Mickey was so inexperienced that he didn't know where to start, but as he was figuring it out, he was surprised to hear Carlie began to sob. He stopped. He had about seventy pounds on her and figured that maybe he was crushing her. He rolled off. It wasn't that. She sat up and wept some more.

"Carlie. Don't. I don't want this." He put a blanket around her shoulders as she composed herself.

She looked at him with new affection in her eyes.

"What's the matter?" Mickey asked, concerned.

"How to start?" she replied. "OK. It wasn't just the dog. I have a startle reaction that's embarrassing. That's why I jumped in the water. I had good reason to be afraid of that dog. There was something worse there this afternoon."

"What was it? You were so scared. It was unbelievable."

"Mickey, didn't you see him?"

"See who?"

"The man back on the shore under the oak trees, with the hat ..."

Mickey stiffened.

"You mean the cowboy."

Carlie nodded.

"The scary cowboy, that's how I described him to the police. His past is connected to mine somehow, it goes further than him seeking me out in Boston. He thinks I'm responsible for his torment, I don't think he'll stop until he has me."

"What can we do? Can we go to the police?"

"The police can't easily perceive him. He's like us but he possesses a dark power. He can shield himself."

Mickey hugged her and pulled the beach blanket tighter around them. "Tell me what happened."

"We lived outside of Boston," Carlie began. "My dad was a scientist, a professor. We lived near Boston because in addition to Harvard, there are a number of almost Ivy League schools in the area. My dad couldn't quite make the grade as faculty at Harvard, but he had become a rising star at one of the smaller competing universities. The cowboy moved in about the time Dad's research began making waves in a select group of scientists around the country. I guess it's my fault. Dad had a Ph. D from Stanford and was doing well in straight ahead biochemistry until I started to talk. The phone would ring and I'd predict the caller. My parents thought it was funny at first."

"Doesn't that happen to everybody?" Mickey said, even though he knew better.

"Not the way it happened to me," she answered. "It was going on all the time and I was starting to develop another strange skill. I knew when I was in danger, or if something was coming to hurt me."

Mickey nodded. "For me, it was calling quarters. But what does this have to do with the cowboy?"

"Well, my dad started to record these occurrences—"

"He didn't use a Big Chief tablet, did he?" Mickey interrupted. Carlie gave him a strange look.

Mickey apologized. "Go on. I'll explain later."

"Well, he started to crunch numbers and look for correlations. After a few years, he ran some analyses of variation and found it couldn't be random. He published an article that caught fire in the parapsychology world. Usually nobody reads those journals, but a Boston newspaper caught wind of the story. I think that's what brought the cowboy to us. The week after the feature ran, the cowboy moved into a rental property two houses down. Three things I'll never forget: he wore a tall cowboy hat, he had a club foot, and he had a huge German Shepherd. The cowboy would walk that dog by my house on a leash whenever I was playing in the driveway. It would lunge at me and bark until my dad came out.

"Then, one day, we saw him hauling his belongings out of the rental unit and piling them into a truck. I still remember the look of relief on my mom's face as he drove away. But that night, our house burned down."

"You lost your family," Mickey said. It was a statement rather than a question.

Carlie nodded.

"When I was old enough to understand, I was told an explosive device had been planted in the crawl space beneath my bed. I know it was him. I am certain in the same way I can predict a phone call. But the police don't have any interest in that kind of evidence. A few days after the explosion, my sense of him went away. I could still feel him, but the signal was obscured. Several months ago it flared up again, like he'd come out of hibernation. The danger is very real."

"'Watch out for the scary cowboy,'" Mickey said, recalling Carlie's words to him back at St. Asors. He turned to her. "Can we be together for a while?"

Carlie smiled sadly and gathered up her things.

"It's not over yet," she said, "I'm still consolidating my power. After I go, we'll find each other again. Don't ask how. You'll know."

They stood up and began to walk. At first, they headed in the direction of her dorm, but after a few steps, Carlie thought better of it and they set off without a heading. Sometimes they talked, but mostly they shared space and exchanged information in their own way. By the time the birds began to chirp and the sun began peeking up over the red tile roof of the old dorms, they knew each other in a way most people don't achieve in a lifetime.

Mickey felt both exposed and fulfilled. They returned to her dorm and Mickey held Carlie in a long embrace.

"You're going again," he stated simply.

Carlie nodded.

"I'll find you when it's over."

"Let me help you," Mickey said. "Maybe together we can . . ." His voice drifted off and he left the idea unsaid.

Carlie looked sad and leaned in to hold Mickey close. Then she separated and went inside. Mickey stood in the soft light of morning for a long while.

He knew she wouldn't be there when he returned.

CHAPTER 21

Wilmington

The next morning, Mort resolved to go back to Madison and finish it.

Sissy was owed that much.

She was owed that much and more.

Mort drove back into Madison to the dorms behind the pier where the previous day's confrontation had occurred. He left Cyclops in the van and walked over to the buildings, peeking around the corner. The guards were out, but no sunbathers. Where could she be?

There was an empty UPS truck by the curb. Mort looked at his own outfit. He was wearing dark brown slacks and a button down gray shirt.

Close enough.

He took off his cowboy hat, grabbed a clipboard off the floor of the truck and a big box that was near the driver's seat. Hoping he would not run into the real UPS carrier, he entered the dorm.

In the summer, the dorms are almost empty with only a few boarders on each floor. There was only one door open on the first floor. He went to it and knocked.

"Package for Carlie Stillman."

A student with her back to the door was listening to Paul McCartney and Wings on a stereo player and trying to read. She did not bother to turn around, but instead looked up and said, "Don't know any Carlie Stillman, but Carlie Tillford is the room on the end next to the bathroom."

Mort thought about this for a second and then smiled. The girl was clever to have changed her name. He backed away from the reclining girl at the door. Speed was of the essence. He scanned the hallway, put his shoulder to the door and broke the wooden frame. He was prepared to grab and go, but the room was empty.

Bare.

She'd flown!

He cursed and turned back, tripping over a trash can next to the door. Mort left the box and the hat and was out of the building in thirty seconds. In his hurry to get to his van, he bumped into a coed crossing the street. She was walking a large tri-color dog. As soon as he bumped into the girl, the dog bit him on the thigh, drawing blood. The curb was piled high with trash left by students cleaning out before they took off at the end of August. Mort cursed and jumped back, tripped and fell next to a pile of discarded odds and ends.

The big dog advanced on him, pulling the smaller coed as she hollered, "Ilsa! Ilsa! Stop! Stay!" Ilsa kept pulling. Mort's hand touched something wooden as he scrabbled backward: a cracked baseball bat. Mort regained his feet. Just as he was about to swing that Louisville Slugger right through the brown and white dog's brain pan, a UPS driver came running out of the building, followed by a girl.

"That's him!" the girl said.

"Hey, you!" said the driver, who was closing fast.

Mort vaulted into his van, gunned the motor and sped off, almost grazing the furious UPS driver in the process.

***

Ten miles away, Mort pulled over at a truck stop to buy a map of the United States. He was furious that she'd escaped him, but now he had her name and the scent of her, that should be enough. The smoke would do the rest. He spread the map down on the table and then put his hands out, palms down as if he were using an Ouija board. His eyes rolled back into his head and the smoke came through his throat and out his nostrils. When he opened his eyes, his finger was pointing at Wilmington, Delaware. Mort nodded, and folded the map before climbing back into his van.

CHAPTER 22

Didn't Think You Had It In You, Brother

Mickey looked around the University of Delaware conference room where the rookie TeachUSA interns were assembled for a two week prep session before being turned loose in the schools. The director, a tall no-nonsense ex-marine, came over.

"Mickey, come meet Mister Dobranth," the director said, leading Mickey over to a tough-looking Polish kid. "Meet Ed. He's from Nazareth, Pennsylvania. I think you two have a lot in common."

Dobranth studied the UW-Madison graduate who had majored in French and extended his hand. "Well, we're the only two Caucasians here, what else do we have in common?"

"We're both warm bodies willing to spend a couple years working in inner city education," Mickey smiled. The director didn't smile; he just made a sharp nod and wandered off. Dobranth and Mickey started to get an inkling of what they'd gotten themselves into. Mickey had a sinking feeling. Throughout training, TeachUSA candidates bunked in university housing. Mickey was assigned to room with Ed.

Racial tensions were thick, and Mickey and Ed got the impression that many in TeachUSA viewed the two of them as part of the problem rather than the solution. Mickey couldn't blame his fellow educators for their suspicions. Somebody had to start taking responsibility and recognizing that racial injustice was an issue. Mickey resolved to do his best to earn the trust of those he worked with and to strive to be part of the solution.

Mickey was assigned to Brunswick Middle School in Wilmington, Delaware. The place was chaotic and run-down. Maintenance was bare bones. The atmosphere had a more oppressive, abandoned feeling than the average county prison. Mickey could not have felt more out of place if he had walked into a Wyoming cowboy bar wearing a tutu and tights.

It turned out skin color was the *only* thing Mickey and Ed had in common. Unlike the psychic pull Mickey felt when he was around Carlie, there was nothing with Ed. Still, Ed was all right, and their lack of a profound connection made him an easy guy to work with.

The members of TeachUSA were told to find lodgings by Labor Day because that was when the university students would be back. They were also told it was expected that the interns would live in the poor neighborhoods where they taught.

Ed and Mickey were dumb enough to believe those instructions. They eventually found out that all of the other interns settled in apartments in the nice suburbs surrounding Wilmington. It seemed that every night when Mickey returned from class, one or two more of his TeachUSA compatriots had moved out from the dorms. Eventually, it was down to Mickey, Ed, a drummer named Todd, and an attractive woman named Karine.

As moving day approached, Mickey began to grow worried. Ed showed no signs of anxiety whatsoever. In fact, he showed no signs of life. It finally occurred to Mickey that Ed's strengths might not lie in the long range planning department.

"Ed," Mickey said, "listen to me. We're being kicked out of here at the end of next week."

Ed was drumming with a pencil on a practice pad. He looked up. "So?"

"So? So! So what are you going to do?"

Ed shrugged and drummed harder.

"Listen, Ed. There's no one left. What say I find a place so we at least have a roof over our heads to begin the school year? If it doesn't work out, we can find other places, but at least we'll be set for the next few months."

Ed put on some earphones connected to his stereo and kept drumming. He was trying to keep up with jazz ace Joe Morello's drumming on *Take 5*. Mickey lifted up the earphones and got a dirty look. Holding up his hand in a peace gesture, he said, "Fine, when you and Dave Brubek are done practicing, I'll be down the hall if you want to talk."

Mickey stepped into the hallway and ran into Karine. She was the group's only Ivy Leaguer and God knows what brought her to

TeachUSA. Neither Mickey nor Ed had spoken a word to her in the two weeks they had all been together.

Karine was great looking, smart, and popular. On the other hand, Mickey's time in exile with Ed had lowered his already subterranean self-concept to precipitous depths. There was a rumor that she coped with it all by being stoned 24/7. Mickey hadn't believed that, but he reconsidered when he saw her wobble down the hallway, gently bumping off the walls. She was tall, with the face of a Vanity Fair cover girl. The walls shook slightly as she self-corrected. She clutched a can of Budweiser, which sloshed a little.

"Hey, Wisconsin, what's up?" Karine said.

"I was wondering where I was going to live."

"Me too. You've got a car. Let's cruise over to the city. Maybe we'll each find something." She held a folded newspaper. Mickey could see she'd made circles on it with red ink.

"You don't have a car?" Mickey asked.

She burped. "I have a Porsche 911. Let's wreck that joke you drive around instead of mine. OK?"

Insulting Mickey's Skylark was not OK, but on the other hand this was an amazing looking woman who seemed temporarily devoid of judgment and willing to go someplace with him.

"Ok!" Mickey agreed.

They hopped in the old blue Skylark Mickey's dad had given him for graduation. He put the top down and pulled away from the curb. It was a short drive down the freeway to the city. Halfway there, Karine put her hand on Mickey's thigh. This was too good to be true!

The first unit they looked at was in a combat zone. Even in her addled state, Karine was perceptive enough to get it. She said, "Don't stop," and crossed that one off. The second offering was interesting. It was in a block of old three-story houses that was halfway kept up. There was nowhere in the inner city that the white college kids were going to fit in, but this neighborhood came close. It seemed diverse in socio-economics and more importantly, children were playing in the street. There was a friendly atmosphere.

"We might not be total outliers here," Mickey said.

Karine let out a horse laugh. "Outliers! What? C'mon, Wisconsin. Are you trying to show off that Big Ten vocabulary? Moo."

The instructions in the paper were to knock on the first floor and get a key. The couple went up and knocked. An ancient woman well into her eighties answered. "Can I help you?"

"We're here about the room."

The woman's expression changed from a look of curiosity to one of appraisal. She gave them both a quick once over. Mickey got the impression that she was from a generation that valued a first impression over any knowledge they could gain from trivial questioning.

"You seem like a nice quiet couple," the woman said. "We need that. My name's Agatha. I live with my mother."

Karine hid her Budweiser behind her Rubenesque hips. Mickey was not going to correct the potential landlady's delusional assumption that they were a couple.

"May I ask," he said, "how old is your mom?"

"One hundred seven. She's got a chance at the longevity record for the oldest lady in Delaware, maybe the world. One more thing. The people on the second floor don't speak English. They are Albanian. Please don't make them angry."

"We'll try not to," Mickey replied.

"You have to go up the fire escape," Agatha said, settling in to a rocking chair just outside the front door.

"Excuse me?" Mickey asked.

Agatha gestured at the steel exterior fire escape running alongside the building. "Take your time."

Mickey sighed and reached for the lowest rung on the ladder. He and Karine climbed up to a door that opened into a small kitchen.

"That's quaint," Karine said.

"Maybe renters aren't trusted to use the interior stairs and hallways," Mickey said with a shrug.

Inside, there was a faint musty smell of a gas leak from the stove, but the place looked clean. Karine looked inside the refrigerator. The previous occupants must have left in a hurry because there were two six packs of Schlitz in the distinctive white and brown cans. Karine took out two, handed Mickey one, popped the top and offered a toast.

"Welcome to hell."

Two hours and ten beers later, hell was a pretty sexy place. They were rolling around on the linoleum, sweating, panting, grasping and a little too drunk to do anything else. Karine leaned up against Mickey and said, "G'nite, roomie." They fell asleep in each others' arms and woke up four hours later with splitting headaches. Mickey's mouth felt like the Russian army had just marched through barefoot. The old lady gave them a dirty look when they climbed down the fire escape, but Mickey knew how to cheer her up.

"We'll take it," he said, and signed the lease right then and there.

The drive back was quiet, but when Karine got out of the Skylark, she said, "I honestly think this might work. Let's spend some quality time together this weekend." She winked.

By the next day, Mickey was rested and looking forward to the weekend. That's when his folks called. His uncle was in town and they wanted the family together. Mickey couldn't say no. They were his folks. And they had given him the Skylark. Mickey agreed, but not without regret. Karine was different than Carlie. Any attraction between the two was purely physical, but what an attraction it was! She had come on to Mickey so hard that he wasn't worried about jeopardizing their get together. He was just sorry to put it off. He left her a note explaining everything, and signed it, "Love, Mickey." Then he tore that one up and wrote the same words, but signed them with 'x's and 'o's.

When Mickey returned Sunday night, Ed looked up from his bunk. "Hey, did'ja know we have to be out of here this week?"

"No shit, Sherlock. That's what I was trying to tell you when you were practicing for the Newport Jazz Festival. It sucks to be you. I went ahead and took care of things. I've got a place … and you know Karine?" Mickey was getting ready to gloat. He couldn't help it.

Ed said, "Oh yeah, that stuck up chick. She is so hot. Hey, this is funny. You won't believe it. She's moving in with that dorky drummer Todd."

"WHAT?"

"Yeah, we were hanging around the lounge with nothing to do. She wanted to know if anyone wanted to go to the beach. He went. When they came back, it was a done deal."

"Why didn't you go?"

"That little Porsche only holds two people and, I dunno, she chose Todd for some reason." He was picking his toes as he said this.

Mickey was stunned. "Todd?" He remembered that moment back in the car when his intuition told him it was too good to be true. Spot on.

"Yeah. And you know what's worse? He came back and started bragging about it. Said she was so horny, they did it right on the beach under a towel. You'd think one of us would have figured out how desperate she was for the horizontal cha-cha."

"Nice metaphor, Ed, but I hardly think that's possible. I spent Wednesday night with her and she's living with me. For the time being."

"Time being zero, Wisconsin. You might want to check out that letter on your bed."

"Ed, this letter's been opened."

He shrugged.

The letter went: 'Hey, Wisconsin. I'm shacking up with Todd for now. Thanks for the trip Wednesday. Good times, right? –Karine'

Mickey flopped down. "I'm so screwed. I put a down payment on this place. I need a roommate. Ed, look at me! Why don't you split it with me? You have to do something."

If Ed shrugged again, Mickey was going to rise above his pacifist leanings and hit him. Fortunately, it didn't come to that.

"OK," Ed said.

Mickey was overcome with relief and in that moment of weakness, he blurted, "You won't regret it. I'll be a good roommate. I promise."

Ed looked up. "Better than nothing. And by the way, losing Karine, I've gotta say, you're a good loser."

"I've had a lot of practice."

***

Mickey and Ed began their lives as teachers. They walked the halls of Brunswick Middle School, two white shadows, painfully aware that they were part of the culture that had ordained the misery of poorly funded, inadequately equipped schools as equal education.

The junior high kids ignored them, backtalked, swore, and treated Mickey and Ed like dirt, but the two young teachers saved themselves by volunteering to coach at the local high school—Ed in football and Mickey in swimming. There, they gained respect from the bigger tougher kids. That support leaked back to the program supervisors who wanted to flunk them out for their ineptitude with the younger students.

Not much else was working for the two roommates until the night of the front yard showdown.

Ed and Mickey had been living together for about a month with little to talk about.

One evening, Ed was preparing to go out by himself for a night on the town. It was warm for the fall and the windows were open. Like the soft breeze floating in through the worn, grease-stained taffeta curtains, the sounds of the city drifted in—the tap, tap, tap of a basketball, followed by laughs and trash talk, the sweet harmonies of the Temptations from the players' boom box, and the squeal of little kids from the playground around the corner. All this was set against a backdrop of the hushed roar of the freeway overpass nearby.

Suddenly, Mickey heard something not so harmonious. Loud cussing, an audible smack and a woman's cry of distress. Mickey leaned out the window and craned his neck to see a commotion near the corner of the house. There was a guy and a girl, and they were hidden from the street and the ball yards by a lilac hedge.

Mickey realized with horror that the man was strangling the woman.

She was a smaller person. His large hands completely circled her throat so that his fingers were intertwined at the back. If he squeezed any harder, he was going to snap her neck like a dead oak branch.

"Hey!" Mickey yelled. The cry came out a lot softer than he wanted. He tried again. It was a living nightmare; the one people have where they try to yell for help but can't make a sound.

Mickey's bad habit of jumping into situations before he knew what he was going to do propelled him down the fire escape and around the corner of the house.

By the time he arrived, the abuser had the woman bent down on her knees in front of him. He towered above her as he continued shaking her. Mickey's bad habit number one segued into bad habit number two, which was never having the right words in a conflict setting. He looked at the girl.

"Do you need help?" he said.

She gurgled something.

The attacker let her go and turned on Mickey. He was not much heavier than Mickey but a couple of inches taller, with rippling muscles so taut and stringy it looked like his skin was painted on. Blue jeans, Baltimore Bullets sweatshirt, and a red bandanna. 100% bad news. The man cocked his head to the side, as the girl struggled to recover her air.

"I'll give you some help," the man said.

Mickey stood his ground, mainly because fear paralyzed him.

The hoodlum grabbed Mickey by the neck.

Mickey had just started to realize he was in over his head when a thunderous "YO!" shook the night.

Mickey didn't dare try to turn for fear of having his throat torn out, but he shifted his eyes and saw Ed charging down the fire escape with a putter in his hand and a crazy look in his eyes.

The assailant recognized Ed meant business. He let go of Mickey and held up his hands. "Whoa, easy brother, be careful with that thing."

Ed arrived at the bottom of the fire escape as Mickey fought for breath. There was no doubt that he was going to commit capital mayhem and the girlfriend saw it coming. She chose her abuser over her rescuer—a scenario the two roommates would grow familiar with over the next year.

"You put that down!" the woman cried. "Someone call the police! It's an attack. HELP!"

She was screaming louder now than she had when she was getting hit.

Ed slowed.

Mickey went to him and put his hands on Ed's arms and got him to lower the club from his Pete Rose stance.

"Ed, it's over. Let's go."

Ed's gaze softened. Mickey turned. Romeo and Juliet were gone.

The guys clanged back up the fire escape. Mickey was shaking so hard that he had to sit down on the top landing. Ed kept going. Mickey figured that Ed was so disgusted by the mess he had caused that he would be going out, maybe even driving home to Nazareth for the night.

He thought wrong.

Ed came back out with a six pack and handed one to Mickey before opening one himself.

"I didn't think you had it in you, brother. That took balls, even if you just ended up getting strangled."

Mickey couldn't help but laugh.

They sat among the rooftops, drinking beer till midnight, swinging their legs, listening to Lionel Richie, and sharing their stories. That was the night the friendship stuck.

CHAPTER 23

MKUltra

Carlie nursed a vodka and 7-Up with a touch of orange juice. The drink was weak, and the melting ice did more to affect the liquid level than the young woman's infrequent sips on the straw. She wouldn't have ordered the drink at all, but the lack of beverage might have been interpreted as an invitation to procure her one. Having the drink deflected certain unwanted attention. Carlie had grown accustomed to hiding in plain sight, in more ways than one.

She sat at the bar of the Elysian Oasis, an upscale place in downtown Wilmington, with four of her male colleagues. It had been months since her rendezvous with Mickey on Lake Mendota, and she hadn't felt any third rail shocks from either her grade school friend or the dark specter from her past. Carlie didn't know what methods either might use to try and find her, but she had done her best to take her own precautions so as to stay hidden.

In her time at Stanford, Gabby had instructed Carlie on the benefits of meditation. Gabby's lessons had been designed only to calm a frantic mind at the end of a day of study, but Carlie had found the mental discipline she developed as a result of her sessions with Gabby helped her peer more clearly into the world of second sight. It was during one of these sessions that Carlie stumbled upon an effect that she came to call 'cosmic static.' By maintaining a deep focus, Carlie found she could diffuse her spiritual essence so as to camouflage her whereabouts from any who might be able to perceive her extrasensory aura. The technique served to turn down the volume on the tingling sensation she felt when she was in close proximity to another person with powers like hers. When she'd first discovered the technique, she had needed all of her concentration to employ it for even short periods of time. Now, however, after years of practice,

Carlie could maintain the effect with the same effort as remembering a list of groceries. She was necessarily self-taught in developing her special abilities, but the fact that nobody had cornered her yet seemed to indicate the potency of her efforts. She often reminded herself that random chance had a terrible way of corrupting all her carefully laid plans. She also knew that when she became scared or agitated, her concentration could slip and then she was vulnerable to a power more formidable than chance.

The Elysian was filled with lacquered wood, mirrors and brass. It was the kind of place that tried to give off the impression of wealth and elegance, but only managed to achieve a vibe of refined sleaze. *Close enough*, Carlie thought. In her short experience as a corporate lawyer, she'd seen wealth and sleaze paired together on more than one occasion.

The other members of the Duchamp legal team glanced in her direction from time to time, but she paid them little notice. In truth, she'd have rather been at home, but she'd gotten into the habit of coming out to happy hour just to keep her colleagues from perceiving her as aloof and mysterious. She preferred cultivating the image of the dedicated workaholic, and sat perusing a set of old case files as her fellow lawyers laughed about who knows what.

"Are you headed to Geneva next week, Carlie?" Nathan asked. He was a middle-aged associate with a jovial air, and was a capable if not passionate lawyer. As co-workers go, Carlie had known worse.

"I haven't decided yet," she said, not looking up.

"C'mon, Carlie, leave the case load alone for a while and relax," Nathan said. There was enough of a hint of genuine concern in his voice to make Carlie cast him a questioning look. Nathan was regarding her with a kind expression.

"I've seen other junior lawyers come in and work themselves to burn-out in less than six months," he said. "Trust me when I tell you that you're doing great work and you can dial it back a bit."

Carlie smirked. "What's the matter, Nathan, are you worried I'll be taking your job soon?"

Nathan laughed. "Ha! You're welcome to it."

"In that case, I don't want it," Carlie replied. She couldn't help but laugh herself as she turned back to her file, but then she saw something that captured her attention. Nathan noticed her suddenly rigid posture and leaned over her shoulder to start reading.

"... in 1946 through Operation Paperclip, the US government successfully recruited approximately 1600 German technicians, ..."

Carlie closed the folder, interrupting Nathan.

"'46, that would mean... the Nazis came to work for the US government? Is that serious?" Nathan asked.

"As a heart attack," Carlie replied, closing the file and slipping it into her satchel. She turned to her drink.

"Wait a minute, what case are you working on?" Nathan asked.

Carlie threw him her most dazzling smile and simply shook her head. Nathan shrugged, the matter forgotten. He opened his mouth, about to change the subject, when a prematurely balding young man intercepted Carlie's gaze and muscled in between the two colleagues.

"Hi there. I'm Marc Winger. I'm an OB-GYN intern."

"Oh God." The words were out of Carlie's mouth before she could think, but Marc took it as praise. He spoke out of the side of his mouth, almost *sotto voce*.

"That's right. Now, how 'bout a drink and you tell me a little about yourself?"

"I have a drink and there's nothing to tell." Carlie tried to look past Marc back to Nathan, but Marc immediately began to grind up against her. Carlie had no patience for such antics, drunk or otherwise. "Keep your body parts to yourself!" she cried, balling her hand into a fist and striking out with all the force of her 105-pound frame. Carlie had never hit anyone before, but she'd done enough yoga and Tae-Kwondo over the years to know how to properly square her feet and get some force behind the blow. She connected squarely with the knot of nerves and cartilage of the hinge joint of Winger's jaw bone. He dropped like a rock, more stunned than hurt.

"Holy shit!" Nathan cried, in a voice somewhere between surprised and delighted.

Winger scrambled up as if he were going to do battle with the tiny woman who had decked him. This outraged her male companions, who were trying to figure out what was going on. One of them was an office mate named Kevin, a gym freak, a three-hundred-pound bench presser. He rammed his open palms against Winger's shoulders, sending him ass over tea kettle backwards over a nearby table. Shrimp cocktails went flying, along with most of the dinner party, and red sauce landed all over thousand dollar suits. People were sprawled on the floor, crawling to get away. The table was overturned and only one small accountant with wire-rimmed glasses remained. There he sat like Little Jack Horner, naked of friends and furniture, all alone on a small chair in the middle of the burgeoning brawl. He put his knees together, lowered his head and covered his ears with his delicate fingers.

Looking for a Pyrrhic victory, Dr. Winger hollered over his shoulder as he headed for the door. "All lawyers are assholes!"

Upscale or not, the Elysian Oasis had a bouncer; a Mr. T clone. He grabbed Winger by the throat and said, "I take great offense to that."

"Don't tell me you're a lawyer too."

"No. I'm an asshole."

Then the bouncer head-butted the disgraced intern and shoved him out the door, where he wobbled headfirst through a group of street kids and landed in the gutter. Back inside, the bouncer spread his arms like a human earthmover and plowed a crowd of writhing, pinching, biting, slapping, squealing CEOs, doctors, and attorneys toward the door. With a grunt, he scooped the mob out onto Market Street. Carlie found herself carried along in the human tsunami.

A taxi driver was waiting for a fare at the curb as the insane surge of clawing humanity rolled out the door. Panicked, he took off without looking in front for traffic.

BANG!

A white van slammed into his front fender and a plume of steam geysered from its hood. Carlie, and everybody else, jumped at the explosive clashing sound of metal on metal and broken glass. She felt herself drawn to the van and raised her head to look for the driver, who was looking back at her from under a big cowboy hat. He had a furious stare. Their eyes locked and Carlie felt a scorch of lightning run down her spine. The driver shook his head as if to bring himself out of a trance. Carlie saw him reach down to open his door. Her heart raced. The air was shattered by a harsh command.

"Wilmington P. D.! Everyone freeze!"

A couple of cops were running up the sidewalk, billy clubs drawn. The van driver ignored the commands and curses of the cops. He backed up, stopped, put it in drive and squealed away, leaving a stream of steaming engine coolant on the road.

Carlie memorized the license plate numbers.

Someone grabbed her arm. She flinched and turned to swing, but it was Nathan. His nose was bleeding and his shirt was ripped open.

"This way!" He ran up the front steps of a brick two-story apartment building. Voices came from behind.

"You two! On the stoop. Stop!" More cops were arriving.

Carlie's escort pushed the door latch. It was open. They ran blindly down the hallway and without thinking ascended the stairwell. On the second floor, they saw no exit signs, not even a fire escape. Trapped.

Nathan pounded on a door and an old man with a US Navy ball cap and a can of beer opened it.

Nathan took out his wallet and said, "Want to make a hundred bucks? Let us in." He waved a Benjamin. Down below, he heard footsteps and then a command.

A voice came from the first floor "Sergeant, I'll check down here. Go look for those two hotshots in case they went upstairs."

Nathan pulled out another hundred. His last. The Navy vet pushed the bills aside and gestured for the lawyers to enter before shutting his door. He opened another door and shoved Carlie and Nathan inside a tiny bathroom just as a knock sounded on his apartment door. It was the cops.

"Good evening, sir. We're looking for two people who started a brawl and caused an accident. They're in this building."

"Not in here, they ain't. I was watching TV and heard the noise. I come running to the window to watch and then you guys came."

The cops looked at his veteran's hat and a framed picture of the USS Arizona, nodded, and said thanks. After they left, the old vet went to the bathroom door and opened it. "It's OK. You can come out. Be quiet. They're still around."

Carlie said, "I'm sorry. It's not what you think. I was …"

"Never mind, little lady. I spent a week in the brig for punching an ensign when we were on shore leave after Tarawa. I didn't start it but I sure as hell finished it. I'm guessin' same thing happened to you. There's a fire escape out my window. You can go down that way."

Carlie said, "Thank you!" and turned toward the window.

"Not now! They're not as dumb as they look. They'll stick around a long time. Come and set a spell. Name's Buck." He gave a half wave at the introduction rather than extending his hand for a shake.

Buck handed them each a can of Ballantine beer and they watched an episode of *Sanford and Son*. When things had calmed down after a little while, Nathan glanced over at Carlie.

"So, tell me what that file is you were working on."

Carlie looked at him in surprise. "It's nothing, Nathan."

"Nothing?" Nathan replied. "Nazis, Operation Paperclip; that's nothing?"

"Paperclip!" The exclamation came from Buck, who virtually spit the word.

"You know it?" Nathan asked. Carlie looked Buck's way as well.

"Darn right I know it, you think I'd forget? I spent four years of my life fighting the axis of evil when as soon as the war ends, we turn around and give those Krauts jobs! The brass thought they kept it secret, but we knew what was going on. How could we not? Half the time we had to work security on those white lab coat losers as they pranced about our ships."

"Security for what?"

Buck put his finger to his nose and his eyes narrowed. "Spooks," he whispered. He took a sip of his beer. "They'd get busted and turn up in the paper every now and then, but you don't stop a spook by busting him. They'd just change the name of their program and carry on: Overcast, Paperclip, Chatter, Bluebird, Artichoke ..." He paused for a moment then whispered, "MKUltra."

"MKUltra?" Nathan said. "That was in the news not so long ago; that was the CIA program responsible—"

"—for the Stanford Acid tests," Carlie said. Buck opened his eyes wide before taking another swig of his beer.

"You can see their thinking, can't you?" Buck said. "Wouldn't it be nice to have a serum to extract information from prisoners? Perhaps an injection to turn high ranking officials against their own government?"

"Jeez," Nathan said.

"But it would all be science fiction," Buck went on, "except for the fact that the Krauts had no qualms about experimenting on human beings. What did our top brass think was going to happen when they absorbed those monsters into our brain circle? Yeah, just a little while after the end of the war, you started seeing news stories about people getting killed while participating in government sanctioned experiments. Some poor fella went nuts and jumped out a window in Maryland. A woman got hit by a bus and killed in L.A. back in '65. Nobody looked into it."

"Why haven't I ever heard of this before?" Nathan asked.

"Well, in '73, Helms, the CIA director, had all the files destroyed," Buck said. "Nobody knows the full extent of what they did."

"Not all the files," Carlie broke in.

The two men looked at her.

"Some were incorrectly stored and were discovered in '77 as a result of a Freedom of Information Act request. I've got copies in my satchel."

Nathan let out a long, low whistle. "Well, you might not have a case file in there, but it's certainly not 'nothing.'"

Carlie didn't reply. She was desperate to control her breathing and calm her mind so as to maybe, somehow, gain some control back over the cyclone that had apparently picked her up. She had little doubt that it was no accident that she had seen the cowboy in the street, or that in their random flight from the cops she and Nathan had ended up knocking on Buck's door. There was some other purpose guiding her, and she didn't like it.

Sanford and Son ended and *Welcome Back Kotter* came on, but the three were hardly paying attention to the television anymore.

"Bad times," Buck said. "I shouldn't even be talking about it, but I don't care. I'm old, I've been lied to enough." He took another swig of his beer, "I'd give out names now if anyone asked. They can all go down as far as I'm concerned; they wore name tags when they came on the ships. Who knows, maybe they were all fake, but I remember them: Cameron, Gottlieb, Stillman ..."

"Stillman?" Carlie said.

"Yeah." Buck leaned back and rolled his eyes into his head, and then looked back down. "Alan Stillman, I think. He was the youngest of them, got in over his head probably, but hell, that's true of all of us."

Carlie said nothing. Buck continued talking, but Carlie could only hear it at a distance. She'd heard enough to shake her to the core and the last thing she could afford right now was to lose her cool again. She remembered Gabby's coaching.

"Breathe Carlie, concentrate on your breathing, think of nothing... think of nothing..."

***

Carlie and Nathan watched TV with old Buck for three hours. When they left, Carlie spontaneously hugged the old man, for the situation had been intense, and he'd been kind to them. Then she and Nathan crept down the rusty fire escape. It made a hideous noise when the last piece unhinged and dropped to the ground, but no one was around to hear. Nathan recovered his car from a nearby parking garage and drove Carlie home.

"Heck of a night, eh?" he said with a wink. Carlie agreed, but she was too dazed to make much sense of the situation.

"Thanks, Nathan, I appreciate you helping me out."

"What kind of stuff are you involved in?" he asked.

"Oh, I'm just a history buff."

"Heck of a history," he smiled.

Carlie thought for a moment and then stepped toward Nathan. He seemed surprised, but wasn't reluctant to have her stand closer. But Carlie didn't embrace him. Instead, she placed her hand on his face with her thumb just beneath his eye and her index finger on his temple. When she was little she had experimented with externalizing her power onto things like drawings. If she focused hard enough, she could put her energy into the carbon of pencil strokes and retain an awareness of them from a great distance. Or even make them move. That had been child's play. She had never even attempted such a thing on another person. She didn't like it, but the risk was necessary. Suddenly, she pushed with surprising force.

"Forget," she said.

Nathan tensed like he was about to protest, but then relaxed. He turned away as if he didn't recognize her, got into his car without looking back, and drove off.

Carlie stood in her doorway watching until the taillights disappeared around the corner, then she went inside. She felt like she was under water: disoriented and disturbed. However, she did not forget to call the police and report the license plates involved in the hit and run outside the Elysian Oasis.

CHAPTER 24

Jail in Wilmington

Mort had searched the streets of Wilmington for Carlie for months without any success. His insight had been no help to him, and that, more than anything, had left him deeply disturbed. He felt a vague, persistent tension in his mind that kept him off balance. She was here, he knew that much, but his orientation spun like a compass in an electrical storm.

He suspected the witch must have cast some sort of restraining spell upon him. How she'd learned to do that was anyone's guess. Perhaps she'd met a guru in the mountains of Tibet. Mort didn't have any idea; it wasn't the type of thing they advertised in the classifieds ... not the real ones, anyway. He couldn't find her. His frustration over her prolonged disappearance seethed. She couldn't hide forever though, sooner or later the force that bound them would make her turn up.

Once again, he'd found work as a roofer, laboring in the hot sun for pennies. He didn't mind the work because it kept him strong; getting paid was just a bonus. He got his real income from muscling people who had it coming.

Then, on a random trip to downtown Wilmington an idiot taxi driver got spooked by a crowd of people emerging from a bar and plowed right into him. Mort slammed on his brakes as his vehicle rolled with the impact and a white plume geysered from beneath his hood.

"Imbecile!" Mort cried, turning to look at the terrified taxi driver cowering in the offending cab. He was set to let loose with a tirade of rage and insults when he saw the crowd of folk emerging from the snake pit behind the taxi. The insults died on his lips. There she was! All this time had passed without any trace and then, out of the blue, she appeared right in the middle of the street. Mort locked eyes with her blank face. She stood staring at him like a vicar caught robbing the donation box for liquor money. People like her were as quick to see the wrongdoings of others as they were blind to their own.

Mort always had a tire iron next to the door. He reached down for it, smiling at its heft. If Cyclops had been with him, he'd have sent the beast running to take her down, but he'd left his buddy back home for the work trip. He could certainly handle Carlie without his pal, but he knew the killer beast would be sad to have missed this. He'd have to be content with the satisfaction of his master. Mort reached down and opened the door when the cop sirens began wailing.

He paused and weighed the risk for a moment before deciding the odds were too far out of favor.

"Damn," he grunted, dropping the iron and putting the vehicle back in gear.

The place was wrong. Mort was a giant and tireless, but even he would have trouble subduing a whole city single-handed. He'd learned enough, this was just the beginning.

He slammed his door shut and hit the gas. As he pushed his truck through the crunched up traffic, he glanced past Carlie to read the name of the bar she'd emerged from.

"The Ely...s...ian Oasis," he muttered, sounding out the words. "I bet you work near here. See you soon, darling."

***

Mort hit traffic on his way back to West Chester where he rented a small trailer, so he stopped for a late dinner before resuming the journey. He was driving slow because the soothing noise of his radials on the highway always helped him think. His thoughts were interrupted, however, when red and blue lights started flashing in his rear-view mirror.

It was dark outside, but Mort could feel the smoke coalesce about him. There was something like a caress upon his cheek. This was no routine traffic stop. Perhaps he'd underestimated her resources. It had been foolish of him to believe she would try to confront him with honor. Mort's muscles hardened in anticipation of battle.

He pulled over and put his hands out the window. The police officer approached.

"Good evening, sir, do you know why I pulled you over?"

Mort shook his head.

"You've got a busted taillight."

"I'm sorry, officer, I'll be sure to get that fixed."

"There's something else. Your plates came up for a pickup truck, not a van."

"I just purchased this car, sir," Mort said.

"Can I see your ID?"

"I lost it."

"Address?"

Mort gestured behind him. "You're looking at it."

Mort didn't have any intention of telling the police about the trailer he'd rented. If they ever did find out about the place, Cyclops was sure to take one or two down to the underworld before he went himself.

"Do you have any weapons in the car, sir?"

An unmistakable hint of suspicion crept into the officer's voice. Mort squinted at the man. Wrinkles around the eyes and gray hairs around the temples led Mort to believe the officer had been on the job long enough to trust his gut.

Mort was about to answer in the negative when the smoke slipped into his throat and spoke for him.

"Yes."

The officer nodded. "Sir, can you take a look to your right?"

Mort turned his head first and then his eyes. Within the shadows and the flashing lights beyond the passenger window was the clear silhouette of a police officer holding a shotgun aimed at Mort's head. Mort smiled.

"If he shoots, he's likely to hit you too," Mort said.

"Don't give him reason to shoot. I'm going to handcuff you now. Don't resist."

Mort tensed, but then the smoke whispered to him again. *No*, it seemed to say, *now is not the time, wait.*

Mort submitted. Neither did he fight as he was led from his truck to the back seat of the patrol car. At the station, they ran his prints and got his name.

"Mortimer LeFrance," the arresting officer said, "turns out you're wanted for questioning regarding a double murder in Indiana."

Mort didn't reply. He stood staring at the wall in his cell.

The smoke continued to whisper to him. Mort listened, now with greater focus than he'd ever had before.

CHAPTER 25

You Had Me There

Mickey's life settled into a steady rhythm. He avoided further domestic disputes and kept his head down at work. He spent a little time playing in a bar band, but got kicked out when his guitar playing failed to improve. One evening, he was sitting around reading Erich Segal's 'Love Story' when the phone rang.

He knew.

He picked up the receiver and said, "Carlie."

"Mickey, I want to see you."

He suppressed his frustration at having gone nearly a year without hearing from her other than a few notes from P.O. boxes in different locations.

"Where are you?"

"In a phone booth, three blocks away. I know where you live."

He wondered how she knew, but his desire to see her overrode any inclination to question. "Please come over. Come up the sidewalk to the fire escape and go up to the top. I'll let you in."

Five minutes later, he heard the rusty old staircase rattle and shake. He opened the kitchen door just as she reached the landing.

"It's been so long, Carlie."

"I know. I can explain."

"I need that. Here I am living in this hellhole, and the only thing that keeps me going is the hope that I might see you again. You look beautiful, by the way."

She did. She had lost some weight, not that she had much to lose in the first place, and cut her hair short in almost a mannish style. The buzzcut accentuated her fine jaw line and highlighted her eyes.

Perversely, his emotions shifted gears. He had an angry meltdown.

"Why are you doing this to me? Don't you realize it hurts to not know where you are? You promised to keep in touch and what happens? I get a random letter saying you're looking forward to seeing me and catching up. You write I'm special and you are lucky to have me in your life. But when I write to the return address, I get the letter back with 'Address Unknown' stamped across the front. You've done that, what, three times since Madison? If you're not going to follow through then maybe you should let me be."

Bluffs seldom work but his words must have had an effect. She hugged him and said, "Mickey, it's for your own good. That guy; the scary cowboy, you called him. I didn't want you involved. It's safe now. He was picked up on a robbery and homicide charge in West Chester. They'll be putting him away."

"What's going on? Why is he fixated on you?"

Carlie hesitated.

Just then there was a crash. The front door was thrown open and slammed against the stove. Something dropped on the floor and broke.

Then came Ed's big laugh, followed by the high pitched, almost hysterical squealing of a woman. There was bumping in the hallway. Suddenly, Ed burst in accompanied by Crystal from the nearby Performing Center. If Mickey hadn't been holding the girl of his dreams, he would have had a stroke, because he had been mooning over Crystal during the lonely months when he had given up on Carlie.

Crystal wore an open trench coat. Beneath it, Mickey could see she wore only her work clothes—a string bikini that left little to the imagination. Up close and personal, her body was even better than it looked from the bandstand.

"Hi," Crystal said, accompanied by a dopey grin. She glanced at Carlie. "Oh, honey, you are so cute. We've got to get you dancing on the pole. I can talk to Art."

"Ed. Do you mind?" Mickey hissed.

"It's ok, Mickey," Carlie said. "There's no reason I can't see you again. We're safe now. There will be another time very soon." She started to get up as if to go.

"Let's have a drink!" Ed said.

For once, Mickey was grateful for Ed's boisterous nature. He grabbed Carlie by the wrist and led her into the living room, serving her a drink before she had a chance to protest. Ed put on his favorite

Sly and the Family Stone album and cranked up the volume on *Dance to the Music*. Crystal started swaying seductively. Carlie and Mickey looked at each other and a strange thing happened. Just as on the beach at Lake Mendota, there was a moment when the clouds seemed to part and they felt safe to relax. Mickey reached for Carlie and the two of them linked in an embrace and began to sway along to the music.

Ed pulled out his snare drum and started banging away, but even that couldn't ruin Mickey and Carlie's moment. Mickey never really got an answer to all his questions, but right then, lost in her embrace, the magic of her presence drowned out everything else.

At about eleven o'clock, there came a pounding on the ceiling below. It was their Albanian friend on the second floor. Ed grabbed the old York barbell with its original 110 pounds on it, cleaned and jerked it over his head and let it drop. There was a thunderous crash, followed by a secondary muffled explosion.

"Ed, I think you knocked his chandelier loose!" Crystal laughed. The next thing they heard was, "I'm calling the police!" screamed up from below.

"Listen," Carlie said, "I'm a lawyer and I think the three of you will now be getting a visit from the cops. Party's over. Good luck. Walk me out, Mickey."

Mickey followed her down the fire escape to her car. They heard the kitchen door open above. Ed and Crystal leaned out.

"Hey! Nice to meetcha," Crystal said.

"Charmed," Carlie replied with a smile. She dropped from the fire escape and startled old Agatha, who was sitting outside as she often did. Mickey watched as Carlie leaned in to whisper something to the elderly woman, who looked up and gave Carlie a warm smile. A second later, Mickey dropped down beside them and took Carlie by the arm.

"Good night, Agatha," Mickey said.

Agatha put her finger to her temple, then looked away. The gesture struck Mickey as uncharacteristically cool for the grandmotherly woman, but in the presence of Carlie he had other things to contemplate.

Arm in arm, the two of them walked to Carlie's car, where she turned and leaned back against it.

"Can't we stay together a little longer?" Mickey said. "We're always interrupted. Let's go somewhere."

Carlie hesitated.

"I'm not going to let you go," Mickey insisted. "I'm going to hold you right here until you agree to take me with you. What are you going to do about that?"

But he did nothing, too timid to act on his threat, uncertain that the embrace would be welcome if he did.

Carlie gave him a peck on the cheek and got in her car. As she rolled away from the curb, she leaned out the window and smiled. "You missed your chance. You had me there. I would have let you keep me. I'll be back though. I promise." She blew a kiss and drove off.

Mickey watched. Halfway down the block, the car's red brake lights came on. His heart fluttered. He ran up, determined not to lose this second chance. As he closed on the car, Carlie stuck her head out and flipped a box out the window, back toward him.

"I almost forgot," she hollered, "that's for you!"

The car's tires squealed and she sped off. Mickey bent down and picked up the small gift-wrapped box. Up the fire escape and back in his kitchen, he sat down at the old Formica table and opened the package the way a child tears open the wrapper on a candy bar.

The box contained a ring.

The ring must have cost a fortune; a simple platinum band. Underneath there was a note.

"Wear this and know that we will be together forever."

Mickey slipped the ring onto his finger and shut his eyes. Now that she was gone, the questions again came bubbling to the surface.

CHAPTER 26

Played

It always took a few days to build a network in jail, so Mort resolved to stay sober for a while. Faced with no means of intoxication and no external stimulation, Mort turned his focus inward. He sat, concentrating on the smoke, slowing his respiration and heart rate so that the mortal world seemed to disappear. Slowly, he began to chip away at the psychic wall that had been erected in his mind. Now that he looked for it, he discovered he had guidance from beyond.

Distractions might have slowed his progress. But there were no distractions in jail.

After a few nights, he broke through, and the smoke swelled around him differently than it had before. Whatever shield the witch had created was destroyed. Or maybe it was extra strength magnified by her proximity. The power felt stronger. Mort's eyes rolled back into his skull and he surrendered to it.

The walls of the cell drifted away and Mort found himself in a city street. It was a run-down neighborhood. A dilapidated apartment building stood before him with a rusty fire escape hanging from the side.

Mort looked around and found a street sign and door number.

The smoke told him it would be worth finding this place if he ever got out.

"Do we go now?" he whispered to himself.

The smoke indicated he should not.

He must wait until news of his arrest spread to the local paper. They'd read it there. Carlie and ... somebody else. He sensed him, the third rail kid from Madison. The lifeguard! They would read about the arrest in the paper and then they'd get sloppy.

You need only wait.

Mort waited a full day, then another. The sounds of shuffling papers and typewriters buzzed in the background, but Mort was in a waking sleep. His eyes darted back and forth behind his eyelids whether he stood, sat or reclined.

Finally, they came to move him. Movement provided opportunity.

They cuffed him first, through the slot in the cell door, then covered his head in a hood. The hood blocked his mortal sight, but not the one that mattered. The darkness closed over him like a womb.

Six men escorted him. Two in front, one on either side, and two in back. Mort observed from beyond as they pushed his body forward. He realized he no longer identified his body as himself. The thing of flesh and bone was just a vessel, a vehicle for his true essence. Still, the vehicle was his, and these men had no right to mistreat it. His escort took him through the office, to the paddy wagon out back. Mort was docile, moving only as they directed, until he felt the sunlight on his neck and wrists.

The touch of the light upon his skin connected him to a strength he had never before known.

Mort's head slammed back into the face of the first guard standing behind him, shattering the man's nose and dropping him to his knees. The two on either side tightened their grip on Mort's arms, but they were no match for the surge of adrenaline and supernatural force that erupted in Mort's veins. He launched himself to the right, leading with his elbow and connecting with the windpipe, then executed the same maneuver to his left. Two more officers crumpled to the ground.

By now, the remaining three were ready. They advanced upon the hooded, cuffed man, confident they could regain control of the situation. But they responded to Mort with the assumption that he was blind, and their error cost them.

Mort moved on instinct. He dodged under their punches and used his shoulder as a battering ram, stomping one of the prone officers along the way. He slipped out of submission holds, ducked haymakers, and brought his opponents down with a defiant mix of physicality, precognition and rage.

When it was over, Mort sat down next to one of the bodies and searched his belt for a cuff key. After his first stint in prison, he'd purchased several set of cuffs and practiced slipping them on and off. The move required only dexterity and deliberate action. These cuffs were different than the ones he'd had before, but he had the smoke to guide him, and soon he'd inserted the key and freed himself from his bond.

Hands free, he pulled the hood from his head and looked about. It almost felt strange to view the world with flesh eyes again. The truck sat not far from him and he still held the set of keys that had opened the cuffs.

He jumped into the car and tried what looked like a car key in the ignition. The engine roared. Mort smiled. He put the police vehicle in drive and a moment later he was cruising down the highway, free and focused on revenge.

***

It took a few days to shake all pursuit, but once he had a little separation he was as good as gone. Somebody had left a sweatshirt in the paddy wagon, and once Mort ditched the police rig, he started hitching. The sweatshirt was enough to disguise his prison issue uniform.

A wood-walled station wagon pulled over.

"Hey, buddy, need a ride?"

Mort nodded and climbed in.

Forty-five minutes later, the car rolled to a stop again and Mort pushed the driver's body into the ditch. He melted the fingertips with the cigarette lighter and stripped the man naked. A couple blows to the jaw from a tire iron and Mort was confident the body wouldn't be easy to identify when it was found.

The pants were good enough to serve as an upgrade for the moment, but the shoes were two sizes too small. It didn't matter; he had enough camouflage to conceal his state slippers now. The image of the city street he'd seen in the cell was seared into his mind and he felt an urgency to go there. He opened the glove box and pawed at the maps, grunting as he discovered one of Wilmington. It didn't take long to orient, and he was back on the road.

It felt strange to come to a place he'd never been but which he recognized. The apartment, the fire escape, the general refuse, all were as he had seen them. A strange feeling came to him, a feeling of vague disquiet. Mort had the sense that something was off, but he couldn't quite put his finger on what it was. He put the car in park and then sat in silence for a long while, surveying the scene like a cat watches a bird. Eventually, he shook his concern away and walked over to the door.

"Can I help you with something?" an elderly woman asked.

Mort seemed to hear a buzzing. It wasn't particularly unpleasant in itself, but it was growing in intensity. Mort looked at the woman with suspicion. She appeared to be in her eighties and was lounging in a rocking chair with a far off look in her eyes.

"No," Mort replied, the buzzing grew louder. Mort lifted a hand to rub at his ear.

Some kids were playing basketball off in the distance. The sound of the ball bouncing on the concrete came to Mort distorted, a moment later, the buzzing drowned it out entirely. Mort lifted his finger to his temple and rubbed his coarse skin with his index finger. He felt a sudden strange pressure. The buzzing became painful. What was he doing here?

"There's nobody in there right now, can I take a message?" the woman said.

She still didn't look at him; instead she stared off into space. Her voice echoed in Mort's mind, barely discernible above the buzzing.

Suddenly he realized; his sight was blocked! He couldn't sense anything. There was darkness all around. How was there darkness? Where was it coming from? What was happening?

Mort took a breath and fell deep within himself. The buzzing throbbed at his temples, but he pushed back against it. He closed his eyes and called upon the smoke. He could sense the other world trying to communicate with him, but the language was garbled. What new witchcraft was this? Had he walked into a trap? Mort felt a need to concentrate. He needed to be alone. Whatever impulse had brought him here needed to be examined and evaluated. He reached for the lowest rung of the fire escape that dangled beside the building sensing a quite spot above.

"Excuse me!" the lady said, still staring off into the distance.

Mort felt a wave of vertigo. His hand clutched the rung tightly, causing the whole structure to rattle. He pitched forward and struggled to stay upright. The buzzing threatened to steal his equilibrium.

"Excuse me!" the old woman said again, this time reaching up to grab Mort's arm.

At the touch of her fingers against his flesh, Mort was struck with an agonizing flash. Like a lightning bolt he saw a vision, and the vision he saw was the face of Carlie, just for an instant, leering before him. He cried out in agony and sank to his knees.

"Excuse me!" the woman said again, emboldened by his weakness. But now the smoke rose up and gave him strength. Mort didn't answer her. Instead, he closed his eyes and could feel the power around him. The smoke urged him to act and he did so without conscious thought. Mort grabbed the woman's arm and threw her into the door as hard as he could. Her head bounced off a piece of stone framework and she began to bleed. She wobbled for a minute before sinking to her knees, and then sat down on the doorstep. There was a lot of blood.

The buzzing stopped.

Instantly, Mort felt the world return to normalcy. The tendrils of smoke freed themselves from the bonds that had restrained them and slithered out into the distance. Mort could see again; a startling realization after such a recent blindness.

With the benefit of his second vision, he comprehended where he was, and all at once the truth dawned on him.

This was not Carlie's home. The face of the room's occupant flashed through Mort's thoughts. It was a young man with curly hair and a quick smile. Mort found himself recalling the beach at Madison and his last encounter with Carlie.

The lifeguard?

What had drawn Mort here?

Through the smoke Mort now caught a whiff of Carlie.

She'd been here.

Her scent was in the room above, he caught her on the fire escape, in the street, but most of all there was a hint of her essence within the body of the old woman bleeding on the stairs.

How had she done this? For what purpose?

Then there came a surge of anger from beyond. A sense of fury that struck like a lightning bolt.

You're being played. All of it, a game!

Mort noticed that everything had gone quiet. The sound of the bouncing basketball had vanished.

Mort whirled and caught sight of kids running off in several directions. They'd bring the cops again! He couldn't stay here. There were too many questions and, for the first time in his life he felt he might be the weaker fighter in the conflict. Panic surged through him, the woman had resources he couldn't imagine. The injustice of it burned him to the core. But for now, the mysteries would have to wait. As fast as he could, the lean biker hobbled back to the station wagon. The engine roared to life and Mort was gone.

CHAPTER 27

Nothing Left To Lose

The days stretched off from Mickey's last hopeful encounter with Carlie, but, contrary to her promise, she failed to come back to him. Her absence hurt him less than it had on previous partings, but what he lost in sorrow he more than made up for in concern.

One night, as Mickey came home, he found his doorway covered in blood. His landlady, Agatha, had been killed in the street.

Some of the neighborhood street kids who played ball with the guys saw it, but they were not much help to the cops. Years of hard-wired fear of the police left them reticent and withdrawn. Charlie, the oldest, spoke for them all and kept it short and sweet.

"It was some weird white dude," Charlie said, "he was kinda tall, really long hair like a hippie. Agatha was telling him to get away from the boys' door. You know Agatha. She don't take no playing around. He ignored her so she got up in his face. And then, man, he threw her into the wall hard and she started bleeding. He ran kinda funny and got in a station wagon and was gone. That's all I know, man."

People were getting killed all the time, but there was something different about this one. Mickey sensed a change. A day later there was a notice under the door that they had to move out at the end of the month. That was fine enough with Mickey; the school year was coming to an end and he sensed he needed a change.

The incident didn't make much of an impression on Ed. During the last month of the interns' service in Wilmington, Ed had found something that Mickey hadn't—a soul mate to keep. Her name was Tracy. She was a social worker, burned out by the same insurmountable odds that had beaten down the young teachers while they were trying to make a difference in the ghetto.

Ed and Tracy met through professional conversations about a child in Ed's class who was being abused.

They got lucky.

The system smiled on them and the boy was removed to a decent foster home.

Their next meeting was at a supper club to celebrate. That was the beginning and the end. It was the beginning of a new and fulfilling life for Ed, and the end of his odd couple existence with Mickey.

Mickey was happy for Ed, but not content with his third wheel status. He was ready for his stint with TeachUSA to wrap up so he could get out of there. He had an offer to continue teaching as regular faculty, but the loneliness wouldn't leave him alone. More than that, he had a sense that he needed to leave. The sense came from a place Mickey couldn't explain. Fleetingly he wondered if he really had any control over where he went or what he did. It always seemed as if he was being maneuvered by a larger force like a tiny piece in a puzzle bigger than he could ever hope to comprehend.

On the last day of school, Mickey had his Buick Skylark convertible packed and waiting. The minute the final bell rang, he hugged Ed, hopped in the car and headed west—destination unknown.

His inventory included: eight hundred dollars cash, a Gibson J-50 acoustic guitar his dad had given him, the York 110-pound barbell set he had had since he was ten years old, and three brown paper grocery bags of clothes.

***

Mickey rode the Pennsylvania turnpike through some beautiful mountain country. There are very long tunnels on the highway and he tried to hold his breath all the way through them to pass the time.

He suddenly felt good about life, now that he had gotten out of Wilmington. It was like the sky had parted and an oppressive cloud that kept the light out had finally dissipated into sunshine. He tried not to think of Carlie in favor of enjoying the uncertainty of the road. Pennsylvania is a long state but he was fresh and doing pretty well. Ohio was not too bad, but by the time he got to the urban mess that starts with Gary, Indiana and runs for a hundred miles south of Chicago, Mickey was beat.

He pulled into a cheap motel outside of Rockford, Illinois. He had planned on sleeping in the car, but he felt a need to celebrate his break for freedom. In the back was a green and white Coleman cooler filled with ice-cold Schafer and a genuine Philly steak sandwich. It was greasy and cold and wrapped in oily wax paper. Mickey took a beer, turned on the TV loud enough to hear and went out and sat on the stoop in front of the motel room, listening to the Reds play the Cubs. Pete Rose was near the end of his career but he had a helluva game.

The next morning, Mickey hit a doughnut store on the way out of town. At 23, health food meant lemon meringue-filled doughnuts instead of cream. He had a thermos of coffee and a full tank of gas. Hours later, Mickey entered Nebraska, the state that never ends. He started daydreaming about Carlie, which got him all the way to North Platte. It had been two years since he spent that chaste, for him at least, evening with her. Then she reappeared in Wilmington and ripped the rug out from under him again. Mickey had to admit he was heartsick. He couldn't escape a funny feeling that she was thinking about him right then, too.

Too much thinking of Carlie was driving him crazy, so he pulled off for a Big Mac and more coffee and remonstrated himself for his mental whining. Was he so special that only one woman on the whole planet could make him happy? It was time to send his thoughts elsewhere for a while.

He drove well into the night, resolving to get the front range of Colorado behind him. As soon as he crossed Loveland Pass, he started looking for places to crash. He turned in at Idaho Springs and stopped at a motel. Before going into the office, he looked at his stash. One night's motel charge would feed him for a week, he figured, so he got back in the car and drove some more, not knowing what to do.

Paying for gas on the way out of town, Mickey thought he'd ask the cashier for advice.

"Any place to crash for cheap around here?" he said, stifling a yawn.

"You got a sleeping bag?" the cashier replied. "This here state is half-owned by the US government. You might as well get some use out of it. Anyplace that is national forest land is free, no rules against camping or whatever. Just look, it's everywhere."

An hour farther on, Mickey turned off near Keystone and started looking for dirt roads. He didn't have to look long. He pulled into one, bumped over rocks and potholes and then parked the car. He pulled out his sleeping bag and spread it out on the back seat. As tired as he was, he could not fall asleep with his knees jammed up against the front seat. He opened the door, threw the bag on the ground, crawled in and fell into a deep and troubled slumber in which he dreamed of big dogs.

***

Mickey woke with a start at daybreak to the sound of barking. At first he thought it was part of his dream, but it was real, and close. He sat up and listened hard. Nothing. Then the sound of a door slamming, and an engine gunning up. A deep chill overtook him, but as the vehicle pulled away and the engine noise faded, he calmed down and stopped shivering. He walked around a house-sized boulder and saw tire tracks in the soft earth, but whoever had been there was gone. He walked over to a small outcropping overlooking a mountain valley. Out on the new horizon, the sun peeked over Mt. Elbrus, the tallest mountain in Colorado.

It took him two more days to get to the Pacific Ocean and he finally started to feel like he had left the past behind. The final night, he pulled off somewhere in the desert in Nevada. His sleep was not good. He dreamed of a man who was tall and lanky wearing black pants, a blue button down shirt and dirty John Lennon-style eyeglasses. He was older, long-haired, but hard looking. He seemed to be searching with one hand over his eyes. In Mickey's dream, the man turned and stared at him. Behind him was a giant dog. Mickey twitched violently and woke up.

Had that vision meant something? He was too tired to decide and fell back to sleep. The image lingered with him, however, and in the morning he decided to pull the Big Chief tablet out of the trunk and write the premonition down. Handling the familiar paper of the tablet took a cloud off him. The present came into sharper focus and the nebulous world of possibility seemed to fade.

Toward the end of the final day of the cross-country drive, Mickey had to decide where he wanted to end up. It had to be the ocean, but there are 2000 miles of Pacific shoreline in the United States. Despite his efforts, he had started thinking about Carlie again. Life had a soundtrack for Mickey. He'd been humming *California Dreaming*. All the leaves were brown. He followed the brown grass hills along the Pacific Highway until he saw a sign for Bodega Bay.

That could be his home for a while.

CHAPTER 28

Pay Respects

Even driving on the poorly maintained Wilmington streets helped Mort relax. The sound took him to another world and almost let him forget that the woman he had killed at the lifeguard's house had left him covered in blood.

Already the stains were going from red to brown. There was too much daylight for him to be seen in public like this. Mort shook his head in annoyance.

He'd given no ID when he was arrested and he'd only been in jail a few days, not so long that they'd think he had split forever. He considered returning to the little trailer he'd rented. He hadn't given a real name to the landlord so they couldn't have made the connection, besides the kind of places he rented weren't prone to checking too hard, but still it was a risk.

He weighed the odds.

With a clean set of clothes, heading back wouldn't have been worth it. But covered in blood, the chances of finding trouble became a push. He decided to take the risk of going home.

The sun was setting as he pulled into the small parking space beside his trailer.

He put the wagon in park and surveyed the scene. Seeing nothing, he switched off the motor and opened the door.

Instantly, a black shape shifted in the bushes.

How did they find this place? Mort thought, as every muscle in his body tensed for battle.

But before he could move, Cyclops burst out of the bushes and ran over to his master, sticking his giant head between Mort's legs and slobbering on his shoes.

"All right, boy, sorry I was gone so long. I guess you are a real badass. Let's saddle up. We got some traveling to do."

Mort rushed through the trailer and scooped up the loose dollar bills lying around—maybe a couple hundred bucks. Then he grabbed a shovel and went outside. He stood on the steps and started at the light pole in the street. He counted off ten giant steps into the yard, stopped, planted the shovel's blade on the ground and pushed it into the soft earth. He dug quickly until there was a metallic sound, then shoveled lightly until there was another tap. He leaned over and pulled out a red Maxwell House coffee can. There were several layers of tinfoil wrapped around the top, secured by a piece of baler twine pulled tight.

The stash represented his savings from assorted robberies over the past year. He shook off the dirt and returned to the kitchen, where he emptied the contents. Over two thousand dollars.

Stripping off his bloodstained clothing, Mort jumped into the shower. It felt good to wash the lingering clutch of jail from his body. He grabbed a new set of clothing, stuffed his cash into a backpack, and then piled everything flammable he could find into the kitchen. He turned on the gas, lit the pile on fire, and then loaded up the station wagon, pausing a few hundred yards down the road to make sure the flames took hold.

They did.

Cyclops climbed into the passenger seat as red and yellow light shot up into the air from the ramshackle trailer.

Mort watched the inferno flicker in the night sky, and even against the backdrop of darkness, he could still see the black smoke rise up into the air. He watched as it rose and drifted off to the west.

"Cyclops, the girl's more powerful than she lets on, she might be too much for me to handle alone." Cyclops turned at his master's voice with an expression that looked doubtful. Mort laughed. "No, I'm not giving up the hunt. But I'm thinking I might have to seek out some reinforcements. Lucky for us, I've got somebody in mind. But first, my mom's buried out in Sausalito. I think it's past time I paid my respects."

CHAPTER 29

Drive Fast and Take Chances

Just south of Bodega Bay there was a wonderful ocean-side park where you could camp and be lulled to sleep each night by the crashing of the waves. Mickey sat on the hood of his car overlooking the ocean and inhaled the wind off the water.

Nobody had a problem with camping, but actually living on the beach was frowned upon. Mickey had no inclination to burn money on an apartment just then. The wind blasts off the sea had the scent of freedom, and he'd live in a cardboard box rather than submit to a lease and live each day counting down to the next time rent was due. So each night, he hid his car uptown and trudged down to the park with his tent.

In the mornings, Mickey woke up early, made coffee and then ran for an hour barefoot on the beach. After the run, he charged into the waves until they were waist deep, pulling him back and forth, then he'd dive forward and swim to a pier about a half mile north where there was coffee and doughnuts. He carried a few bucks in a plastic baggy but they still got wet. That was OK; the owner of the little hut was accustomed to soggy bills.

Back at his tent, he read. He was into Kerouac and the Beat poets, but he also found time for the Big Chief tablet. Although he had resolved to push Carlie from his thoughts, the tablet still called to him. Some nights he considered burning it as if that might allay the hold of whatever paranormal hand had laid its mark upon him. Sometimes he wondered if the hand was holding him back, keeping him down for whatever purpose. Could he free himself through separation?

But he couldn't do it, there was too much of a connection to a past that held hope that he was reluctant to abandon. Even the nights he felt intense resentment towards Carlie, some part of him retained a sliver of affection. Most nights he found himself flipping through the pages of the moments and actions that had gone beyond the easily explained.

'Called quarters with Curly,' read the first entry. 'Curly said I shouldn't mention this ability to others.'

As he cross-referenced his tablet, he noticed a pattern emerge. The instances were always more frequent when Carlie was near. Why might that be? He'd never had a chance to ask her if she could control her abilities. Did she, too, hold them at arm's length, or had she delved into them? Had she explored and found out what she was capable of?

It was generally around noon by the time he could break himself of the tablet. He'd run another half mile, then settle in to sip a few cold beers. Anchor Steam out of San Francisco was the usual. Once the edge was off, he'd wander into town on foot and shop for supper. If he was lucky, he'd find a fishing boat unloading the catch of the day. For a few bucks, they'd grab a fresh fish, gut it in a second, chop it into inch thick steaks, wrap the meat in paper, and flip it down to the buyers on the dock. Mickey would clutch the prize to his chest, jog home, and start a driftwood campfire.

Cooking was simple; just wrap the fish in tin foil soaked with butter and lemon juice and throw it in the fire. A half hour later, heaven would descend upon the earth.

Belly full, he'd watch the stars before rolling into bed. In the morning, he'd do it all over again.

The days were carefree, an intermission between chapters of a hectic life.

Eventually, money became a problem, as it always does.

Mickey was through with teaching. The beach had opened his eyes. If he had to work, he'd prefer doing something that didn't require thought. Sometimes the mind needed to float for a few months or years.

One day when Mickey had jogged into town to move his car, he found a hand-written flyer tucked under the windshield wiper of his Skylark.

'Wanted. Roofers. Sausalito. College education desired.'

Really?

The ad went on to list a phone number and an offer of 'competitive wages.'

Mickey stared at the paper for a moment. Something about it gave him a Big Chief feeling. For a moment, he tried to focus on the sensation, but it slipped away. He felt something like a black cloud pass behind his eyes and whatever special vision he had experienced was dampened.

"Carlie?" he said to himself. Was she out there?

The feeling felt a little bit like her, but also different.

Mickey shrugged.

How could it hurt?

He called from a payphone and was directed to show up the next morning at 7 a.m.

***

Mickey got up at 5 and made the drive to Sausalito in plenty of time. He parked opposite a row of hippie houseboats and walked over to the best little doughnut shop in Northern California. Fueled up and carrying a 16 oz mug of black coffee, he hiked inland two blocks until he was standing in front of an old Sears Craftsman house with scaffolding teetering around the perimeter. There was a black truck with rusted rocker panels parked up in the driveway. It said, 'Nooker Roofing.' Mr. Nooker was in the front yard. He was a tall, gaunt man wearing blue jeans, a white western shirt with the cuffs rolled halfway up his forearms, and a genuine Stetson. He must have gone six feet six, but he could not have weighed more than 150 pounds.

Mickey felt a flashback to the image of the man on Lake Mendota, but the thought left his mind almost as quickly as it entered. He would have pondered the recollection further, but the man in the Stetson hat turned at his approach.

"Are you the guy who called yesterday?"

"Yes." Mickey extended his hand. "I'm Mickey."

"Charles Nooker," the man said, taking Mickey's hand and shaking it vigorously. "Damn glad to see ya. You look like you can handle a bundle; whyn't'cha get started hauling them shingles up that ladder there and stack 'em on the top deck of the scaffold."

It was a big roof. Mickey said, "Ah, Mr. Nooker."

"Call me Chuck."

"Um, Chuck, how many guys are on this job? Just you and me?"

Chuck bellowed a laugh. "Hell, boy! I don't work. I'm the boss, the project coordinator to a college boy like you. You are college, ain'tcha?"

"Well, yeah ..." Mickey eyed the roof and got to the point. "Sir, I mean, Chuck, I'm a pretty good worker but I can't do this all by myself, and to tell the truth, I've roofed before but this old house has some pretty tricky valleys and angles. I'm going to need some help."

Chuck smiled. "I'm just playing with ya, college boy."

Mickey found the moniker was already growing old. "Can I pick my own nickname?"

Chuck looked aghast. "My goodness, such sensitivity. You're right. 'College Boy' does not capture the essence of your being, but we all have nicknames so I'm sure I can do better. How 'bout 'dumbass with degree?' That's it! We can call you 'DAWD' for short."

"Sounds fine," said Mickey, "as long as you don't mind if I call you 'Limp Dick'?'"

Chuck's eyes narrowed and for a moment Mickey thought he might be out of a job. Then Chuck burst out into a noisy laugh and slapped Mickey on the back. "I prefer a man who fights back over one who harbors a grudge. Now that the pleasantries are over, how about we get to work, College Boy?"

Mickey smiled and resolved to just accept the new name.

"I got a master carpenter coming," Chuck said as Mickey pulled on his gloves and went over to arrange the piles of shingles. "He should be here now but he's an ornery cuss. I keep 'im cuz he knows what he's doing, so you'll be ok. But I'm gonna warn you. He likes to get under people's skin, so just ignore him and keep on hauling them shingles up the ladder and setting 'em down for him. You cut 'em and lay 'em out and he'll tack 'em down just right, hear? One more thing. What the hell made you call me up in the first place?"

"The flyer," Mickey said.

Chuck looked puzzled. Mickey continued. "One of your boys must have been at the beach in Bodega because I found a flyer under my windshield wiper."

"I don't have no 'boys,'" Chuck said, "and I didn't make any flyers. Whatever the hell you're smoking, it's a good thing because my other guy's been making all kinds of noise that if I don't get him some help, he's gonna quit, and here you are. What could be fairer, eh?"

Again Mickey paused to think, but found himself interrupted by the arrival of a beat-up Volkswagen van.

"Here he is now," Chuck said.

The gray and black vehicle pulled to a stop and the driver ratcheted the parking brake on with a loud squeak.

Mickey felt the world slow in a way that was both disorienting and unnatural. The sensation was like something he might have recorded in his Big Chief tablet, but at that moment he didn't recognize it as such. He felt seasick, like the ground beneath him was swaying. It was almost as if another power guided his thoughts. Something dark and distant and made of shadow.

A man stepped out of the van. He was almost as lean and lanky as Chuck, but much harder looking. His age was indeterminate. He wore a cop killer Fu Manchu. His face was lined and wrinkled, but he had the body of a man who had done hard manual labor all his life. His large hands were deeply veined and the blue striations were pushed out by lean muscle all the way up his forearms. His thick forehead extended straight up for several inches until it sloped off onto his shaved head. His skin was stretched so tightly over his skull that one could see all the angular bumps and protuberances in sharp detail. He wore strange rectangular glasses that kept slipping down the bridge of his nose.

Mickey felt a wrenching inside. Some instinct told him he recognized this man, but at the same time the warning was pushed back. Again and again the instinct surged, and again and again it was blocked until the notion drifted away and Mickey was left in a state of silent acceptance. Some part of him realized something was off, but his will to question had mysteriously evaporated.

"Hey, Dale," Chuck said. "C'mere. I want you to meet your new help."

As Dale approached, he took off his glasses and tried to wipe the grease smears on his shirt. He didn't look up. He wore a dress white button down shirt and bell bottom blue jeans held up by a belt with a giant buckle adorned with a skull and cross bones. The buttons were torn off his shirt. Mickey stared.

"What the hell are you looking at?" Dale said.

"Nothing." Mickey found himself lamenting the fact that he wouldn't be doing this roof alone.

"Chuck," Dale growled, "this ain't gonna go well if this pissant don't mind his own business." Dale pushed by, and spit some chew near Mickey's shoes. The tall man scampered up the ladder with amazing agility.

Addressing Mickey, Mr. Nooker said, "He don't like to wait. Better strap it on and get hauling."

"OK, but what should I call him, Dale, or Mister …?"

Now it was Chuck's turn to spit. At least he grinned when he did it. "His last name is Graham. He told me to call him Dale. You don't need to call him anything because he's probably not talking to you unless you screw up." Chuck paused in thought for a moment. "You know, 'Sir' might not be a bad choice. Now get going."

Chuck gave Mickey a playful swat with his rolled-up newspaper.

Mickey sighed to himself in exasperation over the situations he got himself into.

***

It takes a lot of older roofers all the strength and balance they have to get even one bundle up the ladder. It was different back in the day in Sausalito. Mickey's regimen on the beach had made him strong and he had the balance and agility of youth. He cradled one bundle under each arm and scooted up the ladder no hands. The effort placated Dale to some extent, and he grunted with something less than feral disgust when Mickey set the bundles down.

Mickey said nothing as he scampered up and down the ladder.

Occasionally, he tried to let his mind wander, but for some reason his thoughts were fragmented and he couldn't seem to focus.

It was a strange day. Dale was quick and efficient and Mickey was strong and willing. By four o'clock, they had half of the roof finished.

At quitting time, Chuck pulled up again. Dale said nothing. He merely scampered down the roof, got into his van and drove off.

Mickey felt a sudden sense of release. He took a deep breath, which Chuck mistook for exhaustion.

"How about a beer, College Boy? I'm buying."

Mickey shrugged and gestured for Chuck to lead on.

They settled in to a beach bar and Chuck's jovial company was welcome after enduring the dark thundercloud of his roofing companion. By unspoken agreement, Dale was not even mentioned.

A few beers in, Mickey realized he had underestimated Chuck. Although Chuck couldn't read the beer list, and he admitted that he only bought a newspaper to look at the comics, he had a vault of other talents. He ran a shade tree garage on the side where he did engine and auto body work. He raised and trained German Shepherds for K-9 service, and he knew an awful lot about guns. His home was inland outside of Novato and he had enough land for horses, which he enjoyed riding. As he described his ranch, he mentioned that beside the horse barn was a smaller barn in which he kept his old single engine Cessna. Mickey was incredulous. He was a pilot too? Mickey was starting to warm to this backwoods Ichabod Crane. Chuck sealed the deal when he mentioned he played bass guitar in a country western band. Mickey offered to buy a round.

Eventually, Chuck slapped Mickey on the back. "It ain't a good deal to get too friendly with the help, so you let me settle up here and you get going. You did good today, but go home and rest up for tomorrow now."

"You don't have to pay it all, let me get half," Mickey protested. "Besides, I don't know if I've had enough yet."

"Listen," Chuck said, "I'm doing you a favor. If you can believe it, they're starting to arrest guys for driving drunk now and I can't afford to lose a good hand to the Marin County Sheriffs. In fact, let me give you a safety tip." He looked away and whistled the barkeep over. "Give me a shot of Jack Daniels and a bottle of Bud, and a six to go for my young friend here."

Mickey started to think he could get along with Chuck. "I thought you said I was going home."

"You are. This is a safety pack. See, it ain't but a six pack to Bodega Bay and if you have this with you, you won't be tempted to stop. Now get ... Oh, and Mickey."

"Yeah?"

"Drive fast and take chances."

Chuck laughed and turned back to stare at himself in the mirror that stretched the full length of the old oaken bar. Mickey looked back as he went out the door. Chuck glanced at the mirror and without turning, lifted his Budweiser in a one-handed adieu.

CHAPTER 30

Backtracking

Carlie knew when he got arrested, and she knew when he got away. She hadn't really expected the bars to hold him; after all this time, she'd come to know her shadow. Whether her intuition was instinctive or extrasensory, she couldn't say, but she'd come to trust her guesses.

The trick with the plates had gotten her one new piece of information when she called the police station after the arrest. They couldn't tell her much, but they gave her a name: Mortimer LeFrance. The name gave her focus, and she was able to use her power to track him. Not precisely, but she had a vague idea of his whereabouts, enough to avoid him anyway.

With Mort on the loose, it was too dangerous to contact Mickey again, but she could feel Mickey out there and his presence calmed her. She also knew he confused Mort. Mickey's presence created interference and without that she suspected Mort might be able to orient on her.

Then Mort disappeared.

Carlie felt it happen gradually. First his presence diminished, then grew smaller before vanishing altogether.

Initially, she thought it must be a trick. Perhaps he'd discovered how to hide himself like she had? Was he waiting outside her door to bury her beneath the earth should she poke her head out from her sanctuary?

She called in sick to work the first day.

But Mort didn't come, and a few weeks later she actually began to hope he was really gone.

Then Mickey disappeared too.

Mickey's disappearance was perplexing. She'd never revealed to him her ability to orient on his location. Mickey didn't have Mort's warrior instincts so why should it occur to him to hide himself? His loss was a more subtle shift and actually made the world darker. Just as with Mort, he slowly diminished before disappearing entirely.

What was going on?

Even as this new mystery presented itself, she was still occupied with the old one. She even returned to talk to Buck to see what more he remembered about MKUltra, but she discovered he didn't have much more to say. He was obviously a lonely old man happy for any opportunity for company, but it became increasingly apparent that the stories he began to tell were just made up.

Carlie was stuck.

She did research on Mortimer LeFrance and found his father had passed away in prison. She requested Lenny's file and discovered his early release from Folsom in '46.

"Folsom," she said to herself.

She pulled out a map of California and took a look. Folsom county prison was only a four hour drive from Stanford.

"A year after the end of World War II," she said. She paused to think for a moment before picking up her phone and calling work.

"Hello, Angie, I'm afraid something's come up and I won't be in for the next week. No, it's nothing major; I just need to take a quick trip to California."

***

The next day, Carlie stepped out of a cab and stood regarding the house of Madame Gabrielle LaJeunesse. A strong surge of emotion welled up in her. This was the closest thing she'd had to a home. She'd felt that Gabby had resented her leaving to some extent, which was both understandable and absurd at the same time. Carlie had sent letters, but after a few years, they'd become less frequent.

Carlie took a deep breath to steady herself, and then noticed that something felt a little off. Gabby's blue Citroen still sat in its accustomed place in the driveway, but Carlie didn't get the feeling of Gabby. Instead, there was something ... different.

She walked toward the door, a little uncertain, stopping only when she reached the small step at the front. She was not one to disregard her emotions when she felt something was wrong, and something was definitely wrong. She paused for a moment, and was about to turn away when the door opened a crack. But instead of Gabby, Carlie came face to face with the figure of an elderly man.

"Hello," the man said, "can I help you?"

He had a swath of white hair surrounding his ears, but was bald on the top of his head. He wore thin rim spectacles and had sharp, birdlike features.

"I'm looking for Madame Gabrielle LaJeunesse," Carlie said, her inquietude rising.

"I'm sorry," the man said, "Madame LaJeunesse is no longer here."

"That's her car," Carlie said, "this is her house."

"Ah," the man replied, "perhaps you'd like to come in for a moment?"

Carlie's alarms were sounding, and she took a step backward.

"No thanks," she said, "I believe I'd prefer to—"

"Are you Carlie?"

Carlie said nothing, but she didn't move farther away.

"Carlie Stillman, correct," the man said, "not Tillford, as you go by? I knew your father. I knew Alan Stillman."

Carlie's eyes narrowed. "Who are you?"

"Please come inside," the man said, "we'd be better off discussing delicate matters where there are fewer eyes and ears." He pushed the door open and stepped to the side, waving the young woman in.

Carlie paused for a moment, but her curiosity overrode her concern. The stranger had touched on the pivotal questions of her entire life. If this man had answers, she had to hear them. Cautiously, she stepped forward, pushing the man's hand away as he went to steady her.

Carlie walked into the familiar room and saw that it hadn't changed much from the days when she used to enjoy a quiet afternoon tea with Gabby. The furniture was the same, but even from a cursory glance, Carlie could tell Gabby hadn't been there in quite some time. Only an old-fashioned leather satchel by the door appeared to be new. Carlie was suddenly possessed by a strong sensation that Gabby had passed away. She was gripped with a terrible sense of loss. The emotion put a crack in her mental control and she struggled to find equilibrium.

"In here, in here," the old man said, gesturing to the kitchen.

Carlie followed and sat in her usual place while the man prepared a cup of tea.

"My name is Doctor Henry Martin," he said with a smile.

Carlie nodded. "I've just been reading a case file that mentioned a Doctor Henry Martin. It was in regard to Lenny LeFrance in Folsom prison back in '46."

Dr. Martin paused but quickly resumed his efforts as if the words meant nothing, but he'd indicated enough to confirm Carlie's suspicions.

"Ah, '46 was a long time ago."

"Yes, you must have been pretty fresh off the boat."

Dr. Martin turned with a much reduced veneer of courtesy. "Did the file you mention indicate the presence of your father?"

It was Carlie's turn to suppress the flicker of emotion from passing across her features. "No it did not."

"Richard Helms was an incompetent idiot," Dr. Martin continued, "or all of the files would have been properly disposed of."

"Yes, you and your kind are quite good at disposing of things," Carlie snapped.

"*My* kind," Dr. Martin replied, "but, my dear, do you not consider yourself to be one of us? After all, so much of our work was made possible by the contributions of your father."

Carlie had become angry enough that she no longer felt the need to hide her feelings. "What was your work, exactly? To dose American citizens with your lab concoctions? To experiment on human beings? To sentence innocent men and women to death?"

Dr. Martin laughed. "Hardly! My goal is to save lives, to preserve peace; it is just as much my goal now as it was then. I'm but a researcher looking for solutions to problems."

"And free will is a problem when it opposes your objectives? How dare you!"

"How dare I? I did only as I was told by your government. They assigned me the task of unlocking the human mind and, don't you see, I succeeded! I did that and so much more. Much more than we ever thought possible. At first we labored only for a truth serum, but then we began to find other things. We discovered how to control the mind, even release powers. Incredible powers. Powers such as yours. Imagine a world where everyone had your abilities, not just a privileged few. Are you really so selfish as to keep your skills all to yourself? Let's share them with the world! But I need to work with you to fully understand what has been achieved and what more we might accomplish."

Carlie's eyes narrowed. "How was it that you didn't take me back when I was seven, when my parents were killed? The paper my father wrote should have indicated I was what you were looking for."

Dr. Martin lifted his hand to his forehead. "Indeed, I was late on that one. I did apply to be your guardian, but by the time the state could provide documentation to approve my immigration status, you'd already disappeared into the system. Your name change made you difficult to trace. I'm glad we can amend that error now."

"No, we will not," Carlie said, and stood. "Doctor Martin, I'm leaving."

"I'm afraid I can't allow that," Dr. Martin replied. "Several of my agents are here and I can assure you we will not fail to resort to using force."

"Force isn't going to help you. You have played with powers you can't possibly understand, and there are consequences to be paid. You've too much faith in government protection, I would have thought your misplaced loyalty to the Reich would have made that lesson clear."

Dr. Martin's face turned into a scowl, but Carlie hadn't finished. "Did you happen to know Oppenheimer? He would have been one of the chief architects of your defeat before you changed sides. Remember what he said: 'I am become death, the destroyer of worlds.'"

"Enough nonsense," Dr. Martin snapped, his face turning into a mask of anger. But Carlie only raised her hand. Her emotion welled up inside her, the loss of Gabby and the anguish from her past combined to assist her in tapping into a psychic energy she had never before felt. The power terrified her even as she barked a command.

"Freeze!"

Dr. Martin froze; in fact, everything froze.

Carlie trembled a little and reached out to the counter to support herself. She took two deep breaths before; she smoothed out her dress and then placed her hand upon Dr. Martin's face. The skin felt harder than it normally did. Carlie pressed her thumb into the space below the eye and affixed her index finger to the temple. Fingers in position, she pushed. This wasn't the gentle wipe she'd applied to her colleague from Duchamp; this was an act of mental violence. Carlie pushed with enough force that she felt the blood vessels rupture beneath her fingers. Still it wasn't enough, and she reached around the back of Dr. Martin's head with her left hand to provide leverage.

"Forget," she hissed, even as her fingers heated at the transference of her power. "Forget everything. When you wake, you will be a baby, you will have to learn again even how to speak. How useful will you be to our government then? I wonder if they'll still take care of you."

When she finally released Dr. Martin, the side of his head was blackened as if he'd just suffered a beating.

Carlie stepped away. As she moved through to the living room, the world began to move again. The power of her charm was diminishing, but slowly. Dr. Martin began lifting his hands to his face, but it would be minutes before his fingers touched his battered skin.

At the entryway, Carlie grabbed the keys to Gabby's Citroen off their accustomed hook. She also slipped Dr. Martin's old leather satchel onto her shoulder.

The world continued to accelerate as she sat behind the wheel of the car and drove away from the former home of Madame Gabrielle LaJeunesse. Stopping only at a parking lot to swap out plates, Carlie hit the open road. There was a hotel up in the Sierra Nevadas that she used to go to for the weekend to escape the pressures of Stanford. It was a rustic place consisting of several private cabins nestled among ancient trees. There was no need to call ahead, the Lenmel Hotel always had vacancies.

CHAPTER 31

Something About Lucretius

The tension between Mickey and Dale seemed to increase despite all Mickey's efforts to be cordial. At the end of a week, there was veritable electricity in the air which made Mickey decidedly uncomfortable.

They had just started in on their third house together. Mickey found himself casting furtive glances at his companion. Something odd was going on and today wasn't the first time he'd noticed. Every time he started thinking about the lean roofer, it was as if he'd lose his place in reality. He'd come to his senses a few seconds later with no recollection of the preceding minutes.

Mickey had done enough roofing to know it was not a good job to work at while you were experiencing momentary blackouts. It wasn't a good job for workplace tension either. The biggest risk came from shingling off the edge. The work keeps moving left to right like a manual typewriter and if one forgets to hit the return, it's the big dip. Such accidents happen more frequently than you'd think. After a couple of hours on the roof, it is too easy to forget that there is a world of verticality around the perimeter of the work area.

The heat of the early morning had just started to come. Mickey was working ahead of Dale. Things were monotonous. Pick up a shingle. Bend over. Place it. Dale stapled it down. Bang, bang, bang. Get a new shingle. Step to the right. Over and over. All with the dark cloud of Dale squatting and scowling in the center of the roof.

Eventually, Mickey ran out of right. He was not careless about this, so what happened next seemed more than an accident. Chuck yelled up something. Mickey couldn't hear him in the wind so he made a move to step closer to the edge and within earshot. He was set to plant his right foot and kneel down, aiming a full foot and a half from the edge. That's when his intuition kicked in. It had been mostly dormant so far in California, which had been part of the appeal of the place. As Mickey bent forward, subconscious red lights went on. Instead of completing the kneel-down, he reversed his forward inertia and straightened up. He planted his legs and pushed hard backward. Just as he did so, he felt Dale's heavy hand plant squarely between his shoulder blades. Although Mickey had never seen him get up outside of breaks, the lean roofer had come to stand right behind him. Mickey's back generated more momentum than Dale's stiff arm and it jolted the tall roofer backward, tipping him off balance. Dale stumbled and fell awkwardly on the roof, spread-eagled and downward. He slid a foot, but then hopped up, his face flushed red. Mickey didn't know what was going on but Dale didn't miss a beat.

"What the HELL are you doing?" he yelled.

Mickey was almost speechless. Images flashed in his mind, and all at once he remembered that day on the beach with Carlie. The memory had been floating just beyond his thoughts, and now it came to him along with the silhouette of a club-footed biker and a large dog. Mickey shook his head to clear it and stuttered, "You ... you pushed me!"

"You crazy, college boy? You heard me say I was getting up for more staples."

Mickey had a habit of grinning when nervous. He was grinning now. Dale loomed over him. "You think that's funny, you son of a bitch?"

"Listen, Mister Dale. I didn't think any of that was funny. You had your hand on my back. That's a fact. That's a push."

Dale was starting to overheat. "I had my hand in your back because YOU. BACKED. INTO. ME. YOU DUMBASS!"

Mickey became confused, and he felt a cloud pressing in on his thoughts. What was going on? This was more than just a workman's quarrel. Just then, Chuck clambered up on to the roof.

"What's going on?"

Dale answered first. "College boy was trying to be cute and he bumped into me backward. Now he's claiming it was an accident."

What was there to say? The fact was that Mickey did back up before Dale touched him. How was Mickey supposed to tell Chuck that, without looking, he knew a push was coming? Being raised Catholic has distinct disadvantages, like a hyperactive conscience and a proclivity for second guessing oneself. Mickey also knew better than to discuss his powers of intuition.

Dale capitalized on the younger man's indecisiveness. "You see, Chuck? The little genius is confused. Can't talk his way out of this one." Then, to Mickey, "I oughta put a dozen of these staples right into your forehead, you little smartass."

Mickey was looking for a way out. He turned to Chuck. "Can we just get back to work?"

Dale spat and walked to the far end to start another row. Mickey raised his shoulders in a 'What was all that about?' pantomime. Chuck answered with a shrug of his own and said, "Time for a frosty." Then he scooted down the ladder and headed directly to his cooler and pulled out a beer. There was the snap of a poptop. Mickey descended the ladder and walked off to his car.

Mickey was thoroughly confused about who did what, but not about his course of action. He did not know the source, but the altercation had started his intuition to ding and light up like a pinball machine. He would have to watch both guys like a hawk, finish the job and then get the hell out of Sausalito. He resolved never to work with either of them again.

On top of everything else, Mickey also noticed that Dale was laying the shingling wrong.

Maybe Mickey was feeling a little hot headed after the pushing incident. After the break, Mickey decided to tempt fate and broach the subject of shingle placement with Dale. The top half of a shingle is a continuous piece. The bottom is actually split into three sections called tabs, separated by about a quarter inch gap to help water run off. The shingles are supposed to be laid in such a way that the tabs from the shingles above and below do not line up vertically. To do this, you cut off half of the end of every other line of shingles. This alternates the placement of the tab. It prevents erosion of the shingles from water run-off. Mickey was shooting for extra credit on this one, because Dale had yet to speak one word since their run-in. He had almost managed to kill Mickey, and now seemed to have decided to adhere to a no comment policy. The roofers got to a roof edge pretty quickly and Mickey decided now was his moment.

"Say, Dale?"

Dale never looked up, he was used to Mickey setting the shingles down and he merely reached back with his right hand, waiting. Dale wiggled his fingers in a come-hither motion.

"So Dale, can I ask you a question?"

Dale sighed urgently and loudly, as if he needed to let off some pressure from frustration before he would explode. Even Chuck, down on the sidewalk flirting with a female mail carrier heard it. Chuck turned, looked up and gave a 'don't do that' kind of wave with both hands. Too late.

Dale shook his head, and then rolled over from his knees into a sitting position. Then he spoke. Finally.

"What?"

That was a start, Mickey proceeded.

"So Dale, I was reading that if you don't alternate the placement of the tabs…"

Dale fiddled with his knee protectors and then picked at a hangnail, and finally put his head between his hands.

"Well, alternating the tabs is better. It helps the water run off. I just have to hand you shingles with the proper tab cut. It's no extra work for you." Mickey finished. "So, what do you think, Dale?"

Dale clenched his jaw. "Are you done?" He rolled back over and lifted his hand again for a shingle. Mickey placed a shingle with the proper tab cut. Dale looked at it strangely, stood up, stepped back and stared at it.

Mickey was suddenly aware that Dale was very tall. The stillness was broken as Dale exploded into motion. With a violent backhand of his long arm, he Frisbeed the shingle off the roof and into the front yard. Then he took his power nailer by the air hose and began swinging it like a cowboy about to lasso a steer. Mickey backed up as the orbit of the heavy tool increased its apogee and velocity. Dale let it go. His deranged space experiment whistled past Mickey's head toward the Pacific Ocean until it abruptly came to the end of the hose, at which point the heavy nailer was yanked back and down to the ground. It crashed onto the front of Chuck's truck, knocking off the three-foot-wide Texas Longhorn their boss had bolted to the hood.

Dale advanced on Mickey. For a minute, it looked as if the tall roofer was going to charge. Instead, he did something even scarier. He yelled. More than a yell. A preternatural scream that turned heads for blocks. The vessels on the side of his temples popped out like purple worms. His face was tomato red. Then there was a sonic explosion from his mouth: "Well, I guess I don't know a damn thing about roofing!"

Then, Dale jumped off the roof. They were only one story up, but it was still a fifteen foot drop. Mickey gasped, figuring they would be calling an ambulance, when the strangest thing happened. It was over in an instant, but it seemed as if Dale slowed in mid-air. He landed in a light graceful crouch like a cat. Mickey wouldn't have believed his eyes if he had not recognized the action. Dale had sailed through the air exactly as Mickey must have looked back on William's basement stairs. As Dale rose from his lithe crouch, he seemed more animal than human, but then he was back to himself and he limped over to his van. The worn shocks on the driver's side compressed as he got in and turned the key. The van revved violently. Over the roar of the engine, it sounded like he was yelling.

Dale put the van in drive and held the brake. When he let go, the van shot forward like a jet catapulted off an aircraft carrier. He barely made the turn at the corner.

Chuck looked at Mickey. "What d'ja do?"

Mickey tried to explain as Chuck climbed the ladder to help him finish the job. But Chuck eventually waived him off.

"Relax kid, anyone could tell old Dale was a bit unstable. Let's just get this roof done and we'll plan our next step after that."

It turned out that Chuck was a pretty fair carpenter, faster than Dale and a helluva lot more sociable. When they got to the first roof edge, Chuck held out his hand like Dale had, but he said,

"You're right, of course. Dale messed up those tabs, but it'll be years before it'll make a difference an' you an' me'll be long gone."

"So why didn't you make him do it right?"

"Mickey, we were getting the work done and I figured I'd drop him pretty soon. 'Course, I been saying that to myself ever since I hooked up with him."

"So why'd you put up with the guy?"

Chuck looked as if he was going to tell a larger truth, but instead he just said, "It didn't seem like a good idea to fire him."

They finished the job and went to have their usual beers. Mickey had the sense that Dale would not return, and without the specter of the tall roofer hanging over him, Mickey suddenly felt a sense of relief.

But Mickey had been spooked by something he couldn't quite put his finger on.

"Chuck," he said, with the kind of tone that made Chuck pay attention, "I like working for you and I'd probably stay a bit longer, but things are getting a little weird around here and I think I've got to get out."

Chuck took off his hat and ran his fingers through his hair. "I'm already short a man, Mickey, can't you stick around a little bit? I can do a little better with the money if that will make any difference."

Mickey smiled in a kind of sad way. "No, it's not that, Chuck." He paused for a moment as if deciding whether or not he should say what he was thinking. Then, all at once, he polished off his beer, and turned to Chuck conspiratorially.

"That Dale gave me a bad feeling."

"I hear you, son," Chuck replied, "he was an ornery cuss."

"No," Mickey said. "I mean a really bad feeling, and when I have a feeling, it means something."

Chuck twisted his eyes in confusion.

Mickey cracked open another beer and took a long pull. For the first time in many years, he decided to go against the advice Curly had given him back on his front porch in the summer of '69.

"Do you have a quarter?"

A few minutes later, Chuck was regarding Mickey with a new kind of respect. Calling a flip thirty straight times had provided enough evidence at least to put his disbelief aside while he heard Mickey out.

Mickey told the whole story, starting with St. Asors all the way to the present day. He told about Carlie, about his premonitions, and about how every time she got close, something conspired to spirit her away. At the name of Carlie, Chuck eyes lit up. When Mickey explained how she changed her name to Carlie Tillford, Chuck stopped him.

"I've met her," Chuck said.

It was Mickey's turn to be surprised. "You met Carlie?"

Chuck gave Mickey a slow nod.

Even for a person who was used to living with strange coincidences, Mickey was flabbergasted. "When?"

"A few years back, she came around asking questions about my daughter R—" Chuck's voice cracked. He collected himself and continued. "My daughter Ruth."

"Your daughter?"

"My daughter disappeared years ago, Carlie thought she might have an insight."

"Did she?"

"I don't know," Chuck replied. "We're caught up in something it seems. The threads of fate have spun us together. But it remains to be seen who is the spider and who is the fly?"

Chuck slouched back in his chair, nursing his beer on his belly as he tried to come to terms with the strange revelations they'd just shared.

"You know," he said, "I wondered why a college boy like you would be out puttering about on the beach and scrambling around on roofs when you clearly had better opportunities. I figured you'd probably had your brain scrambled by a woman somewhere. I see I wasn't wrong."

Mickey glanced up in surprise.

Chuck grinned. "I can't call quarters like you, but I've had plenty of women play head games with me."

"Carlie isn't the problem," Mickey said. He would have continued but Chuck interrupted him with a laugh.

"Isn't it funny how the thing you're looking for is always in the last place you look?"

Mickey didn't understand.

Chuck took a drink and then raised his hand. "Let's not have an argument. Love blinds a man to logic. But hopefully self-preservation will kick in and you'll realize trouble's afoot. The truth will be made plain for you when you're ready to see it. Enough talk of heartache; let me make you a deal. Tonight, you go home and sleep on it. Tomorrow, if you want to work a bit more, you still have a job but with a fifteen percent raise. There's no need for rash decisions. Let the summer play out a bit more. Go out, meet some new girl, take her on a date. Forget the past. Carlie sounds like trouble to me. Take it from this old roofer; you can cover up old mistakes with a new line of shingles." Chuck finished his beer before adding, "And by 'shingles' I mean 'girls.'"

Mickey couldn't help but laugh, and he was still laughing when he crawled into his tent back at Bodega Bay.

CHAPTER 32

Satchel

Carlie drove straight through, only stopping for gas on her way to the Lenmel hotel. She felt a need to go there, not necessarily because she thought she'd be safe, but because that was where she felt she needed to be.

Her mind was racing as the sky darkened and highway lights came at her like a pack of hyenas.

"Gabby," she whispered as she drove, trying hard to keep the tears away. On any other occasion, she'd have been running to Gabby's house after a spook like this. But Gabby was no longer available.

Her brief interaction with Dr. Martin had revealed much, but so had her touch upon his face. Never in her life had she come into contact with such pure evil. She shivered as she drove, the reflexive motion traveling down her arms and into the steering wheel. The car wobbled, but Carlie corrected and continued on her way.

Touching Dr. Martin, had revealed an overwhelming sense of obsession. She saw flashbacks from his childhood, to his days of study, and finally his opportunity to work on human subjects. There were also images of him searching for her! Little had she known that the camouflage she had adopted to fend off Mort would also work to dissuade other faceless enemies. How many more were out there?

Carlie felt the bile rise in her throat.

The US government had given him his opportunity, not some foreign power; the supposed "land of the free and home of the brave" had conspired with Nazis. How far her heroes had fallen.

The worst was that it had all been right there. Anyone could go into a library and do the research. Strange stories of government experiments that ended in the loss of life. They sprang up throughout the years, and somehow people just accepted the official explanation and went on with their lives. That was easier she supposed. Easier than questioning the indomitable force. They were all too saddled with paying student debt or hospital bills to have time to contemplate the greater conspiracies that surrounded them. The mass of people just kept their heads down and tried to survive. That was probably all by design as well.

A semi flew by in the opposite direction. The driver was laying on his horn and the noise was a discordant wail that woke Carlie from her reflections. She glanced over to her right and saw Dr. Martin's satchel sitting in the passenger seat of Gabby's Citroen.

Would the answers to her questions be contained within? Or would it be a collection of new and even more terrible horrors?

Oddly, ever since she'd been in California, Carlie had the sense of Mort and Mickey once more. Muted, but present. Now that she was driving away, the sense of tingling ambiance was fading once again.

"Mickey," she said to herself, hoping that he was safe.

Did Dr. Martin have more agents in California? For, of course, he couldn't be the only one. There were always many; like a hydra, you cut a neck only to have two more grow back. The ones who fell to the darker impulses of human nature sprang up like weeds in constant need of pulling.

Carlie sighed.

The road stretched on before her.

***

It was mid-morning by the time Carlie pulled into the Lenmel hotel. The establishment had a central office, but was composed of various cabins scattered around a secluded area. The office manager regarded her.

"Hello, Miss," he said, with a good dose of country charm. Carlie smiled; the jovial attitude was the type of small kindness she desperately needed.

"Got any cabins?" she asked.

"Of course," the manager replied, "it's a week day, there's not a lot of demand for recreation during the week. Coming up for a few days of R&R?"

"Yes," Carlie replied as she filled out the paperwork. When she was done, she smiled, took the key and headed out to Cabin 1.

Cabin 1 had a living area, two bedrooms, and a small kitchen. It was a nice little vacation escape. Outside, the cabin overlooked a lake with a small pier. There was even a canoe moored to the pier for residents who wanted to come up and fish.

She brought Dr. Martin's satchel inside and set it on the small table in the center of the kitchen. Then she took a seat on the other side of the room. For a while, she regarded the satchel as if it were a dead animal defiling her living space. The item reeked of its owner's evil nature. No small part of her wished to take the repugnant item outside, build a fire, and watch it be destroyed. But she knew there was too much important information contained within.

Steeling herself, she stepped into the kitchen, opened the worn flap and pulled out a stack of papers.

Many of the papers were photocopied forms that had been filled in with sharp and precise handwriting. There were also pages of notes written on yellow legal pads, but these were written in German, and Carlie's German was not good enough to make sense of the writing. Carlie deduced that the photocopied forms were bureaucratic reports. As lenient as Dr. Martin's superiors were about having former Nazis come and perform experiments on US citizens, they wouldn't allow those same scientists to submit their results in anything other than English.

"You can wear the constitution as a diaper with hardly a whisper of reprisal, but fail to stand and respect the flag ..." Carlie shook her head in disgust at the logical distortion. Icon worship somehow always superseded the adherence to fundamental principles. There was even a commandment to that effect, but people were prone to failing the tenets of their religion as often as the fundamental principles of their nation. Carlie continued her musings as she pushed through the papers, but then she stopped and lifted a document from the pile.

'Subject #23: Leonard LeFrance—Folsom Prison 1946. Subject is a poorly educated, foul-tempered individual with a remarkable constitution. Was administered dosages of increasing potency throughout the scheduled test period. SUBJECT SURVIVED though the dosage was elevated to three times the level which had proved fatal in other cases. Subject's resilience allowed him to achieve qualification for early release. MONITOR!'

The form was stapled to a series of further reports. Carlie paged through them one at a time, scanning from top to bottom, not really sure what she was looking for. It was not until she reached the fifth page that she paused, and suddenly sat paralyzed except for the shaking of her hand.

Down at the bottom of the report a second signature began appearing next to that of Dr. Martin.

Project Coordinator: Alan Stillman.

Carlie recognized the elegant looping swirls of the handwriting, as identifying as a fingerprint. There could be no doubt. Her father had played a part in unleashing this abomination upon the world.

CHAPTER 33

Reunion

A feeling awoke Mickey from his ten beer slumber.

There was something outside his tent. Whatever it was hadn't made any noise, but Mickey knew it was there. That third rail tingle ran up his spine. Mickey felt a strong awareness that he was in great danger. He shouldn't have stuck around an extra night. He should have climbed into his car and driven until the tank ran out of gas, and then he should have started running.

Why hadn't he?

He knew the answer; something had compelled him to stay. There were always other forces at work guiding and manipulating him. He caught fleeing glimpses of them sometimes as they scurried off into the shadows.

"You're awake," a voice said. Mickey recognized the words as a statement rather than a question. It was Dale's voice. A sense of hyper-awareness came over Mickey. His mind reached out for anything in the tent he could use as a weapon, but he found nothing. He did, however, feel a growing sense of agitation outside, so he decided to answer.

"Yeah. What are you doing here, Dale?"

"Open the tent."

"I'm putting on my pants first."

Dale said nothing.

Scrambling into his clothes, Mickey reached for the zipper and pulled the tent flap open. On instinct, he grabbed his Big Chief notebook, not really sure why he'd done so.

It was late, but the moonlight was sufficient to highlight Dale's lanky, muscular frame leaning against a tree. Dale looked like the man Mickey had been working with the last few days, yet at the same time, something had changed. Mickey blinked. It was as if a veil had been lifted from his perception. He gasped as his vision cleared and the smoke that had been confounding his memories evaporated into the shadows.

"I recognize you," Mickey said. "I've seen you before."

"Took you long enough," Dale replied.

Mickey squinted. "You're the cowboy from the lake, you're the one Carlie fears; your name is ... Mortimer LeFrance."

"Yup, college boy, Carlie and I go back a long way."

Mickey's body seemed to understand there wasn't much use in being afraid, so he adopted an air of strange calm. He still sat in his tent as he regarded Mort.

"How did you disguise yourself from me? I can usually see more than others do."

"I know, I can sense that on you," Mort said. "All our powers are growing, mine, Carlie's, yours. But at the same time something's holding you back. Haven't you noticed?"

"What do you mean?"

"You're susceptible to influence," Mort stated. "It's not surprising, since Carlie's been working a spell on you for decades. That's why I keep running into you; don't you realize? She keeps spelling us together. You are the distraction to keep me at arm's length."

Mickey's jaw tightened but he had no inclination to provoke the tall and dangerous stranger. All his senses, both real and extrasensory, told him that Mort was a very dangerous man. The best course was to get all the information he could and bide his time until a favorable moment arrived. The more they talked, the longer any physical altercation could be avoided. Mickey knew his intuition would be there to help him should it come to a fight, but the outcome was uncertain. Mickey preferred not to take the risk.

"Where else have we met?" he asked.

"Delaware."

Mickey's eyes widened in understanding. "My landlady, Agatha, you killed her ..."

"I threw her into your doorway and she started bleeding. Old people die, that's not my fault."

Mort's words enraged Mickey but he fought back any kind of retort. Instead, he reflected on what he had been feeling about the time of Agatha's death.

"I left Delaware after that," he said, "I was compelled to leave. I just loaded up and hit the road. I want no part of this." He risked a look at Mort, who stood there nodding. "I see now that I sensed you then and wanted to get away. Why didn't I sense you at the work site?"

"I blocked you, it's a trick I learned in jail." Mort took a step forward. It was the slow step of a laborer, a man who could walk all day and drink all night. Mickey was fully aware the man could pounce on him at any moment, but he didn't believe Mort was going to. Not right then anyway; the gnarly roofer had larger ambitions than murder at the moment. Recognizing this fact did not put Mickey at ease.

A few steps away, Mort squatted down.

"I'd given up after Delaware, you know. I have the same compulsion as you. Something always whispers to me where I should go and what I should do." He picked up a stone and tossed it into the long beach grass. "After ... what was her name?"

"Agatha."

"Right," Mort said, pointing, "after Agatha was discourteous enough to bleed all over me and the entryway to your house, I went home, gathered up my things, burned my trailer, and decided to go and pay my ma a visit."

"Where does your mother live?" Mickey asked.

Mort smiled.

"She's dead. She's been dead a long time, and it wasn't fair the way she died. You see, a bunch of college kids pretended to be her friends."

Emotion came over Mort, and he paused to collect himself. As much as he feared the man, Mickey recognized the pain flashing across his face was genuine.

"College kids like you," Mort resumed, his voice trailing off. "Now, let me explain the type of person my mother was. She worked very hard, harder than any college kid ever had to. My dad wasn't good to her, in ways that soft college kids can't even imagine. She was a sweet woman and she took care of me, and she shielded me from as much harm as she could. She took those lashings upon her own flesh until I was big enough to take them for her and eventually stop them. Our lives got better then, for a little while, until, like I said, a college kid pretended to be her friend."

Mort shifted.

"She should have known better. I told her so. But when you've been as low as my mother, you become desperate for any chance to climb a bit higher. So even though she knew not to be vulnerable, or to believe what was too good to be true, and to keep her defenses up, she let hers down. Only for a minute, and the next thing she knew she was getting dragged beneath a bus with her hair wrapped around and around and around the spinning transmission."

"I'm sorry," Mickey said.

Mort grinned.

"Well, that makes it all OK, doesn't it? Great seeing you, buddy!" He stood up and slapped Mickey on the shoulder. Mickey tensed, but no further blow came. Then Mort spun around and walked over to his vehicle where he stopped and opened the door.

"Get in."

Mickey coughed.

"I don't understand, Mort, what has this got to do with me?"

"What does your intuition tell you?" Mort asked.

Mickey shook his head.

Mort came back over to stand in front of Mickey with considerably more malice in his gait.

"I left Delaware and I would have been content to never see you, or anyone, ever again. I'd left it, as much as I have a legitimate claim. I left. I traveled across the country, found a job, settled in, and I'd not worked for more than a week before who should arrive but a little old college boy from Madison and Delaware."

"It's just a coincidence," Mickey replied.

"You don't believe that. Coincidence doesn't exist for us. We may not know each other, but something within you is connected to something within me. Even if we haven't crossed paths physically but for a few times, your life has influenced mine. We're like celestial bodies passing through space; never touching, but pulling one another to some grand inevitable cosmic destruction. Somebody is pulling the strings."

Mickey's heightened awareness went into overdrive, like what he sometimes felt when he was around Carlie. The ticking rhythm of the world seemed to slow. He became aware of the minute details around him. He could feel the multitude of grains of sand upon his arms, and could distinguish the individual blades of grass that the wind whispered through."Can it not be a harmonic convergence?" he asked. "Must it be destruction?"

Mort shrugged. "I'm not making the rules here, college boy. Were that the case everything would be much better for me."

He stood.

"Now, come on, we've got a long way to go."

Mickey knew there was no point in resisting. There was no point in running. He quickly ran through several scenarios in his mind, but his instincts told him they would fail. He had to go with the lanky roofer who'd already once tried to kill him. Even if he did escape, the roofer would come again.

If they were celestial bodies, their respective orbits had decayed. They'd plummet together now, plummet into the atmosphere to be consumed by flame in a spectacle of death.

Mickey clutched his Big Chief notebook, then stood and walked over to the van. Mort glanced at the notebook but didn't object; other than that, he hardly looked at Mickey. Mickey knew there would be weapons inside Mort's van, and the terrible, muscular dog that sometimes pursued him in his nightmares. But he was trapped.

He climbed into Mort's vehicle and closed the door.

"Where are we going?" he asked.

Mort smiled.

"What does your intuition tell you?"

Mickey closed his eyes and inhaled. He let the breath out long and slow.

"No answer, college boy?" Mort chided. "Maybe you ain't as smart or as talented as I'd been led to believe. Didn't you ever learn anything about gravity? Celestial bodies exert a pull upon each other. When one goes, they all go."

"Carlie?" Mickey said.

"Yup, she's the key to unlocking this riddle. She's avoided a collision until now, but her time is long past due, and with you beside me, I can find her."

CHAPTER 34

Road Trip

Mort and Mickey drove in uncomfortable silence for hours, semi-hypnotized by the sound of the road and the blue moonlight reflected off the pavement. It wasn't until the light of dawn began to crest the horizon that Mort deigned to speak.

"What's it like for you—the feelings you get, your power? I haven't had much chance to discuss this with anyone who'd know."

Mickey kept his eyes forward. Mort was a shadow in his peripheral vision; a dark, immobile mass, terrible and unpredictable. There was energy between the two of them, a horrible power. Mickey had once had a scrap of metal torn out of his hand by a junk yard magnet. What he felt now was not dissimilar. He was connected to his imminent reality in a way he'd never known.

"I don't have much control over it," he said. "Sometimes my body reacts. Like when you tried to push me off the roof."

"I had to see what you were made of didn't I? If my perceptions were correct, you weren't in any danger."

"And if they weren't?"

"But they were," Mort growled in a tone that indicated the discussion had ended.

Mickey regarded Mort out of the corner of his eye. There was a console between the two of them and on top of it rested a ball point pen. Mickey shifted his focus to the pen in an effort to distract himself from Mort.

The pen had a white body and a blue cap. It was of the cheap variety you bought in packs of fifty. The sight of the common object brought memories back to Mickey that were a welcome diversion. He thought of St. Asors and Sister Angelica, who always had a pen like that on her desk.

He thought of Carlie.

Instantly, his musings were interrupted by what felt like an electrical burn. He turned his focus back on the road ahead and tried to clear his mind. However, one thing had not escaped his notice. The pen had moved! Not the random jostling from hitting a bump on the road. The pen had, ever so slightly, levitated before falling back to the console.

"For me, I'm pulled places," Mort said, oblivious to the dancing of the pen. "I'm given directions, told what to do, and I follow." He snorted.

Mort contemplated for a moment.

"I've crossed the country many times. These roads call to me. Whenever I'm uncertain, I get a vehicle and set sail on the highways." His voice was gravelly and trailed off.

Mickey nodded. He could understand that, at least.

As he sat beside Mort, Mickey's discomfort didn't ease but his fear did begin to ebb. He felt like a child who had fallen into a tiger's cage. The tiger was a beast of pure physicality that could not be beaten by force. The tiger was also a pure killing machine that could not be reasoned with. But the tiger had other impulses too, and buried deep beneath the cruel exterior, perhaps there was a sense of solitude that could be exploited.

"I've crossed the country many times, too," Mickey said, "it feels like you're voyaging through space. Sometimes the night highway is the only place I can be alone with my thoughts. Nothing encroaches. Perhaps it's the sensation of motion that eases a troubled mind. The dark parts are soothed by the thought that you're doing something— even if the action doesn't fundamentally bring you any closer to your goal."

Mort said nothing, but he didn't seem to object either.

"What is your goal?" Mickey asked. "Where are we going? Or do you not know?"

"Oh, I know," Mort replied, "or something knows. I'm being guided. The impulse is stronger now that I have you beside me. The message is clearer. All my life it's as if I've heard the murmur of words whispered too silently to comprehend. I think those words are the secret. They need to be magnified only the slightest bit and all will be made clear."

"But how might you magnify them further?"

"By bringing the three of us together, that enhances us."

Mickey blanched.

Mort noticed and smiled.

"She's orchestrated a lot of this, you know. On several occasions she's gravity whipped us all out onto distant, separate paths. But such manipulations only delay the inevitable. We've both been pawns in her game."

"No," Mickey said, "I don't know what you're talking about."

Mort laughed. "How chivalrous, the noble knight protecting his lady. Let me stimulate your memory. She was with you at the beach in Madison. She was with you at your place in Delaware. When she's with you, the pull strengthens and I come like a moth to a flame. Carlie Stillman is the one behind it all. You know her. She's been using you."

Mickey was beset by a mixture of emotions. Anger, pain, and confusion all tumbled upon him in too great a tangle to sort through in that vulnerable moment. He pushed the issues aside, finding that he needed to respond to Mort because silence would betray more than he wished to reveal. "I don't hardly know her," he admitted. "You're right, she's been there, she's circled me like you, but I've rarely seen her. I've talked to her a few times, and I know her only as I know you—as a force beyond my power tugging me in directions I can't go."

"Ha!" Mort said. "Lovesick, eh? What grand illusions have you painted upon her? Pathetic. Don't you know what she is?" His voice grew deadly.

Mickey didn't answer.

"Tell me this; has she brought you any good?" Mort asked. "Or does she only give your heart enough time to heal before stepping forward and ripping it out again? She's a conniving manipulator."

"I don't think so."

"Then you're blind. Would you be here with me in this truck if not for her? Examine your life. Did she make it better? You're intoxicated, boy. She's done nothing but play you since the moment you met her. What importance do your emotions have for her? There's a promise of heaven, yes, but what has she given you really? What tangible evidence of her affection do you have? Nothing! Nothing but heartache and longing. Don't be fooled by your own good nature. Don't project your goodness onto a dark thing."

Mickey stared ahead. The sun poked through the darkness and shone into his eyes. He squinted the painful light away. Chuck's words came back to him about the ability to perceive the truth only when he was ready. Could what Mort was saying be true? Mickey felt a cold hand clutch at his heart.

"My mother was the only good person I've ever known," Mort said. "People like us have a sense for goodness, like how dogs instantly know whether or not a person they meet is somebody they can trust. They all know. For all the intelligence of men and women, they can't pick a good person as well as a dog. The evidence must be obvious, for a dog's judgment is unerring. Yet most people are blind."

"Good people don't kill," Mickey replied, allowing himself, in his anger, to provoke.

Mort shook his head. "That's where you're wrong, college boy. There are murderers that need to be killed by good men. There are pedophiles and slavers and rapists that need to be killed. There are people out there who prey on the weak and torment them, and experiment on them like they're animals. Those people must be slaughtered by good men."

"Like Agatha?"

"Did you know Agatha?" Mort returned accusingly, and he gave Mickey a look so intense the young man couldn't match it. "Did you *know* her?"

"She was my landlady," Mickey replied, "she was taking care of her mother."

"Answer me this; how did you feel around her? Did you go and visit her in the mornings and have coffee? Did you while away the evenings chatting with her? Or was there something about her that made you scurry by? Some sort of sense, like a dog might have, that there was something off?"

Mickey took a breath.

"What are you saying; that she was evil? That you killed her to rid the neighborhood of a foul spirit?"

Mort shrugged.

"You should check the papers and see what kind of shape Agatha's mother was in when they found her. It's not so uncommon for children to hospice their parents out of a need for vengeance rather than affection. The circle is completed. An abused child remembers the pains inflicted by an all-powerful parent. When the parent becomes powerless, the pains are repaid."

Mickey found he couldn't immediately refute the statement. Had Agatha's mother been suffering torment in the rooms beneath Mickey's floor for the year he'd lived there? The thought made him sick.

"It's true I've killed a lot of people," Mort continued. "None of them were innocent."

"You tried to kill me," Mickey said. "What did I do?"

"Like I said, I was testing you, if I'd been trying to kill you, you'd be dead. I might add that I sensed the stain of her on you, it confused me. Maybe she put it there. When you dodged, the stain was displaced. I noticed the displacement and didn't finish the job. I had to think about it for a while. I let you go."

"I found footprints outside my tent."

"Yes, I'd come to visit you many times. I might have shot you or cut your throat in the night. But always I was unsure, always something stopped me. I felt as if I was being toyed with. So I left a note upon your car so you'd come closer and I could learn the truth."

"That was you?"

Mort nodded. "I waited, and now you live and sit beside me."

"Why are you after Carlie?"

"Because she's evil," Mort said simply. "Dogs don't like her. You've seen that; they growl when she's near."

"Only your dog."

"You're blind, college boy; she's cast a spell on you. She's retarded your development in life for her own gains. I've lifted that spell. Can't you feel a difference?"

Mickey took a deep breath. Though Mort's presence was oppressive, there was a part of him that had felt lighter since he'd come. The strange calm that allowed him to master his fear. Could both the fear and the calm have Mort as a common source? The line of thinking troubled Mickey, so he pushed it aside.

"What did she ever do to you?"

At this, Mort's eyes narrowed and he clutched the steering wheel so that his knuckles turned white. "Her parents ran an experiment on my mother. My mother was a lab rat to them. I warned her. I warned my dad, but they wouldn't believe. They wanted so much for the attention and the affection to be real. They killed her."

"But even if that's true, that was Carlie's parents, not Carlie."

"Carlie's cut from the same cloth. The same darkness runs in her. Don't try to pigeonhole this conflict into common law. We're celestial creatures, you and I, and even her in her own dark way. We have our own rules, our own means of torment. I must be rid of the curses she's placed upon me."

Mort's conflict swelled within Mickey. He tried to push it away, but the rage and terror and dark longing grasped hold of him on a profound level and caused him to doubt.

"Don't pretend you don't suspect her guilt just a little bit. I can feel it in you. You're sick of the way she's manipulated you," Mort said.

"So what's going to happen?"

"Isn't that obvious?" Mort replied. "We're going to find her and you're going to help me kill her."

CHAPTER 35

Convergence

A combination of Mickey's presence and Mort's inherent power directed them to a small cabin in the woods of the Sierra Nevadas. Mickey watched the headlights illuminate the winding dirt road until Mort shut them off to drive by moonlight.

A cabin appeared in the darkness, a Citroen parked out front. There were no lights on. Mickey's intuition was setting off alarms. There could be no doubt Carlie was inside.

Some distance away from the cabin, Mort switched off his van.

"Open the door slowly, and leave it open. If you slam it, or make any noise, there will be consequences." Mort lifted a pistol. Mickey could see that he had an additional pistol stuffed into his belt.

Mickey slipped from the van and left the door open behind him. He clutched the Big Chief notebook nervously, drawing strength from the familiarity of the soft, worn cover. He began to walk in the darkness of the woods. Deep down, he understood that no matter how this night turned out, his life would never be the same.

Mickey knocked on the door, Mort standing behind him with the pistol pointed at his back. The night sounds of the woods surrounded them.

As Mickey waited for Carlie to open the door, he couldn't help but wonder what the expression on her face might reveal the moment she saw him. Would she be surprised? Angry? Concerned? What would her expression mean? After all, this was the first time he had sought her out. Always before, it had been Carlie dictating terms.

The door cracked open and Mickey found himself staring into those same pretty blue eyes he remembered from St. Asors.

"Mickey?" There was an edge in her tone, something unexpected. Mickey would have reflected on it further but Mort pushed him forward. The chain on the door broke and Mickey fell into the room. Carlie stumbled back to avoid him, and then she looked up. Her face went pale.

"You," she said.

"Hi, Carlie," Mort said, "it's been a while."

Carlie tensed, but it didn't take her long to realize there was no place to run. Her eyes narrowed. Mickey felt a brief paralysis that passed almost instantly. Mort's eyes widened at the sensation but he, too, was not overly affected. He laughed. "Paralysis? That's a good trick; I bet it works wonders on common folk. Not much use on us though. Where did you learn that? Let's have a seat, why don't we? We have a lot to talk about."

Mickey was still on the ground, getting slowly to his knees. He stood and regarded Carlie.

"You brought him to me?" Carlie asked, her voice a mixture of fury and betrayal.

"No," Mort replied with a tone of condescension, "you brought *me* to *him*, let's not confuse things. Now, sit down!"

The last was an order and Mickey and Carlie sat.

The table was of old-fashioned design with a flake print on the top and a silver trim along the borders. Mickey sat down and laid his fingers on the surface. Carlie did likewise across from him while Mort made himself comfortable at the end.

"It's been a long road to finally bring us here, eh Carlie?" Mort said.

Carlie said nothing; she was fixated on Mickey. Mickey found he was still having a hard time reading her gaze, but he thought he might have detected sorrow there.

"Hey," Mort said, "kid!" He slapped the barrel of his gun on Mickey's head. Mickey winced at the blow. "Don't let her bewitch you!"

"What are you talking about?" Carlie said.

"Oh, quit the games, doll face," Mort snapped. "I told him your whole con."

Carlie looked utterly bewildered, but Mort just laughed. "You're a pretty good actress."

"Mickey," Carlie said, turning back to the young man, "I don't know what he's talking about."

Now it was Carlie's turn to get a slap from the gun barrel. She winced, grabbing her head with both hands. Mickey flinched.

"Enough," Mort said. "No more lies, I won't have it. I've told him all about the marks you've left, the crumbs you've cast behind. All these years, you've used this one as a decoy. Every time I've gotten close to you I've ended up with him. Don't try to sit there and tell me it's by accident. You've put some sort of hex on him to dull his abilities."

Carlie turned her gaze to Mort. "You're insane, I don't know what you're talking about! I don't know what you mean by 'marks.' I don't have that kind of control!"

"Ha!" Mort barked. "See how she gives herself away, kid? She claims not to understand, yet right away she recognizes I'm talking about her power!"

Mickey began to suspect something. With shaking hands, he put his Big Chief notebook on the table and opened it to a back page to reveal a drawing of a little girl's face. In the image, the figure held her finger up to her lips and in a comic strip balloon coming out of her mouth was written, "Shhhhhh!" Mickey reached out to touch the drawing and felt a distinctive electric shock. Instinctively he jerked away and swiped at the Big Chief notebook so that it flew across the room. Throughout the years he had never dared touch the drawing, yet he always felt a need to hold the notebook close.

"I never knew where that image came from, I'd lost my notebook and it was there when I recovered it." Mickey looked up. "Did you draw it Carlie?"

Carlie's face went white and Mort roared approval.

"You see?" Mort said.

"You don't understand," Carlie pleaded.

Mickey felt conflicted. Was it true? Had she left signs for Mort to follow?

"At Lake Mendota," Mort said, ticking the instances off on his fingers, "Delaware, the apartment ... I've always been drawn to you and found him! Let the poor guy off the hook, Carlie, you've only sought him out when you sensed I was getting close."

"No!" Carlie said. She began to cry, but Mickey noticed she couldn't meet his gaze.

"Carlie," he said, "Carlie?" Still she refused to look at him, even when a note of tenderness entered his voice.

"It goes even deeper than that, doesn't it, girl?" Mort continued. "Did you ever tell your little lover boy here who your father was?"

"Yes," Carlie said, seizing on a positive answer, "my father was a research specialist for Stanford ..."

"No!" Mort roared. "I'm not talking about his cover, I'm talking about his actual job."

Carlie looked confused. "He had no other job!"

"Check his resume, there's a gap between 1946 and 1949, what did he do then?"

Carlie shook her head.

"Don't tell me you don't know!" Mort cried. "I don't believe it. He might never have told you, but you're smart enough to have figured it out!"

"My dad was doing research for the government on the effects of LSD in association with—"

"We all know about how your dad killed my mom. I'm talking about the other work. Who was interested in the LSD, what purpose did they have, and, more importantly, what was their greater mission?"

Again Carlie seemed to draw a blank. Mickey couldn't read her. The situation was too charged, too emotional, his intuition taught him nothing. He cast about for answers and his focus came onto a pen sitting on the table. The second the object caught his eye, he saw it move.

"To what purpose?" Mort continued.

Carlie was shaking her head, and the gesture infuriated Mort.

"To create us, you idiot! You know that the CIA was involved with the Stanford tests. They thought they could use LSD for interrogations or some such nonsense. But that was only a small fragment of their ambition. What they really wanted was a way to probe an enemy mind. Think of the ramifications."

"Weaponized psychokinetic abilities?" Mickey asked.

"Give the college boy a cigar! I'm glad they taught you something. Is it so hard to believe that they'd be doing research on such things? Is it so hard to believe that they'd recruit scientists with an interest in a background in chemistry to try to augment any naturally occurring result?"

"Dr. Martin," Carlie stammered, "I've met him. That's the enemy. He's the one you want. My father didn't ..."

"Where was he in 1946?"

"I don't kn-"

"Folsom County Prison!" Mort cried. "Not as an inmate, but as a doctor. A CIA employed doctor supervising the administration of injections to prisoners. You know who else was in Folsom then? My father! A year after his little reunion with Alan Stillman, I came along, and lo and behold, I can see things that aren't there."

"Coincidence," Carlie stammered.

"I swear to God I'm going to hit you again," Mort replied, but he was animated and undeterred. "I don't think he got any good results from that first batch, nothing besides me anyway, but I wasn't what he was looking for. My dad never showed the slightest ability and old Alan probably never bothered to follow up on the havoc he had wreaked. So it was back to the lab for another go around. You'd already probably come along by then. Who knows, maybe he mixed up tinctures and poured them in the public water supply, which resulted in lover boy over here." Mort gestured at Mickey. "Maybe he mixed up these tinctures while he was watching you, Carlie, and perhaps he forgot to wash his hands before mixing up your bottle."

Carlie shook her head at the accusation but she had started to hyperventilate.

"Then again," Mort said, pleased he had unnerved her, "he's always been a bit careless with your well-being. The scientific paper he wrote on you shows that much. I wouldn't be surprised if he added his tincture to your baby formula deliberately."

It was time for Carlie to get physical; she took Mort by surprise and slapped him hard across the face. Mort snarled and reached across the table to grab a handful of Carlie's hair. The situation would have deteriorated if Mickey hadn't stepped in.

"Stop!" he bellowed, with such force that the windows rattled in a way that indicated more than just the power of voice.

The struggling pair paused and looked over at him. Mickey was standing, his fists clenched.

"Stop!" he said. "Not like this, Mort."

A sneer curled up Mort's lip, and he tossed Carlie's head aside as if she disgusted him.

"What are you proposing, kid?"

"Time is a river, and whatever clues we might have found have already passed, but that doesn't mean there shouldn't be some sort of accountability."

"Keep talking," Mort said.

"A game," Mickey replied, "I propose we play a game."

"What sort of game?"

"Put a bullet in your revolver, spin the cylinder, then we'll pass the piece around. Let's let fate decide. One way or another this needs to end."

"No!" Carlie yelled. "Mickey, that's madness."

"Shut up, Carlie," Mickey snapped. Carlie looked more wounded than she had when Mort grabbed her hair. "There's more truth to what Mort says than you're letting on. I've been blind to that before, but I'm sick of being played."

"No ... no ..." Carlie whispered.

"But we'll be able to see where the bullet is," Mort said.

"You know as well as I do that we can block each other," Mickey replied. "It'll be a fair game. Let chaos finish this."

Mort was smiling now. He leaned back to show the other gun in his belt, then opened up the cylinder of his revolver and let the six bullets drop onto the table. He selected one, gave it a kiss, and then loaded it into the weapon. Spinning the cylinder, he looked at Mickey.

"Who is first?"

"I'm surprised you'd have to ask that, Mort," Mickey said. "Ladies first, you know, in honor of your mother."

Mort's features whitened ever so slightly, then he smiled again and turned the revolver over to Carlie.

"Go on, Carlie," Mickey said.

Carlie was terrified. "Mickey, Mickey, I never left 'marks' for him to find you! What I put in the notebook ... it was to protect you!"

"It's OK, Carlie."

"Mickey, I never wanted this, I wasn't using you!"

"It's OK, Carlie," he repeated.

"I'm getting bored," Mort snapped.

"Carlie," Mickey said, "relax; the odds are better than a coin flip."

The words stabilized Carlie. She put the gun beneath her chin. "I'm sorry, Mickey," she said. Then she pulled the trigger.

The cylinder turned and the hammer came down with a snap.

There was no explosion.

Carlie let out a gasp of relief.

Mort snorted.

Mickey reached for the gun. Mort only smiled as the younger man took the weapon and put it to his head.

He closed his eyes and thought of Curly sitting outside on the shady street of his small suburban town. Once again, he could hear Curly's voice.

"Call it in the air!"

Mickey closed his eyes and pulled the trigger.

The hammer clicked against the empty chamber.

Mickey sighed, opened his eyes, and pushed the weapon over to Mort.

"Now you," he said.

Mort hefted the gun and put it to his temple. "So it comes to this, does it?"

Mickey nodded. "We've all taken our turn, the fates haven't spoken yet."

"Oh, I think they have," Mort replied, "you know as well as I do that the next chamber has the bullet."

"What?" Carlie said.

"Yeah," Mort replied, still holding the gun to his temple, "he has kept a few things hidden from you too, doll face. I could see where the bullet was the whole time and I think he can too. For a minute there, I thought we were working together. I guess that's not the case."

"There are still empty chambers. Pull the trigger, Mort," Mickey said. "Finish the game."

"So you're still on her side, eh?" Mort replied. "Pity, I thought I'd made you see reason on the ride over here." Mort moved as if to take the gun away from his head but found that he couldn't. Carlie watched as Mort began to strain against an unknown power that was holding the gun to his head. She turned to look at Mickey and was shocked to see his face tight in concentration.

"Don't do it, boy!" Mort growled suddenly realizing the game of chance had been a deception. The real play had been to get the barrel of the gun against his temple, "don't do it! She's the one, Mickey; it's her, you know it's her." He shook himself backward and forward, twitching madly in every direction. But the gun would not be dislodged, and now Carlie could see that Mort's finger was tightening. The movement was very subtle, but she could see the muscles swell as, bit by bit, the trigger was pulled ever inward.

"No, release me, don't do it, it's her, it's he-"

There was a terrible explosion and a spray of blood erupted from the side of Mort's head. The lean biker's inert body slumped onto the table.

Mickey sat and stared as blood poured out of the wound and onto the white table top with the cheap gold flakes. Soon the blood was pouring down the sides along the silver trim. Some of the blood got on Mickey. He didn't move, uncaring.

"Oh Mickey," Carlie said, "did you do that?"

Mickey replied with a slow and deliberate nod.

"But how?"

"I first noticed at Lake Mendota," he said, "I saw a pencil move there. That's only ever happened when I was close to you. Around both of you, the ability was even stronger. I noticed it growing on the drive up here. I don't think I could force an arm to the head, but I was fairly sure I could keep one there if it went on its own. I knew I could force the finger."

"Mickey," Carlie said haltingly. She pushed her chair back from the table and came over to grab Mickey in a warm embrace. But Mickey stopped her.

"Wait," he said.

"But Mickey, Mickey, you don't believe him do you, you didn't believe him ...?"

"It's not that," Mickey said. "I understand that you have some things to say, and I know we have much to talk about, but a man is dead and I need to concentrate on that for a while."

"Ok, Mickey," Carlie said, "Ok."

CHAPTER 36

Maybe Vegas

Max and Eugene were the two deputies on duty at the Lenmel police department.

"When was the last time there was a homicide in Lenmel?" Max asked.

Eugene was the senior officer. He took a sip of his coffee and leaned back in his chair. "It was during my first year, almost forty years ago. A kid got mad at his parents. Killed them both, put them in the freezer, and then hosted a party at his house."

Max let out a low whistle. "That was a strange one last night. It was odd to find those two kids just sitting there with that body bleeding all over them. You'd think they'd have got up and moved ... tried to clean themselves off or something."

"Who can tell in situations like that?" Eugene replied. "Human beings are not equipped to handle such things; not the innocent ones, anyway."

"You think they're innocent? What if it was just an act?"

Eugene shook his head. "Their behavior was too weird to have been a show. Who thinks of that? Who thinks of just sitting there quietly covered in blood waiting to be discovered? They were in shock."

"I don't know, it seems suspicious to me."

"Well," Eugene answered, "we'll find out in a minute. I faxed the prints of the corpse to the FBI, we'll see if anything hits."

No sooner had he said this than the fax machine sprang to life. There was the sound of a dial-up modem, followed by the grind of a low resolution dot matrix printer. A coil of paper began to turn up on the top of the machine. Max walked over and took a look at it.

"Looks like our body has a bit of a record," he said.

It turned out to be an understatement.

Twenty minutes later, the coil of paper was a couple feet long and not showing any signs of stopping. Felony after felony was listed, followed by a list of open cases where Mortimer LeFrance was listed as the chief suspect.

Eugene took a look at the file and then shook his head. "Max, go and let those kids loose. Tell them their story has checked out."

***

Mickey and Carlie found themselves in the semi-deserted parking lot of the Lenmel police department. Gabby's Citroen was parked out front; the cops had brought it over after the office manager had called in the gun shot and they'd been discovered with Mort's body.

The two of them stood in the brutal morning light. Mickey shielded his eyes with his Big Chief notebook. Carlie was the first to speak.

"Mickey?"

Mickey reflected how there was a time when the sound of that voice would have brought tremors to his skin. Now, he almost wanted to block it out.

"Mickey," she asked again, "will you please talk to me?"

"Things are different now, Carlie," he said. "What happened last night isn't the type of thing you can just forget. It doesn't matter if it was justified or not."

"But we're free now, Mickey."

"Are we?"

"What do you mean?"

Mickey pulled a folded piece of paper from his pocket and handed it to Carlie. At first she was confused, but as she opened it she realized it was Dr. Martin's report on Leonard LeFrance.

"You left that on the table," Mickey said. "Mort was focused on you and I stuffed it in my pocket before he noticed. Once the police put us in a cell, I had plenty of time to read it. That's your father's signature at the bottom, isn't it?"

"Mickey," she said.

"It's OK, Carlie. You weren't even born then, after all. What fault lies with you?"

Carlie sat down on the curb.

"Are you angry with me?"

196

"Just give me a minute," Mickey said. "I have to think about things. Can't you see I need a moment to process this? I'm involved here too, you know."

"I know," she whispered, "I'm sorry."

Mickey sat down on the curb himself. He took a deep breath. A distance larger than the length of the parking lot divided them. They sat in silence for a while.

"You know what I'm tired of?" Mickey said finally.

Carlie didn't answer, just shook her head.

"I'm tired of scrambling around on roofs and teaching in the inner city and never having enough money. I think I'd like to go back to the beach and live next to the ocean and forget the world for a while."

"That sounds wonderful," Carlie replied. "We can do it now, Mickey, I have plenty of money."

"No," Mickey said, "I'm not going to be dependent on you."

Carlie looked away.

Mickey dug into his pockets. He came up with about forty dollars. He looked at it sadly, then turned to Carlie.

"I tell you what," he said, "now that there's only two of us, I don't know if I have the same abilities I did last night." He paused to think for a moment, then fixed Carlie with a serious look. "But I bet with enough time and the proper amount of concentration, I could still influence a roulette ball."

Carlie smiled. "You know, I think you probably can."

"How about giving me a ride to Vegas?"

"Absolutely."

Decided, the two of them stood and walked in unison to Gabby's Citroen. They opened the door, took their seats, started the engine, and pulled out of the Lenmel police department. In unison, they rolled down the windows, then noticed the parity of their actions and laughed.

"The road has always soothed me ..." they said together. Then stopped and smiled. Much of the tension had dissipated.

Mickey regarded the road before him. He didn't know where it might lead and that suited him just fine. Mickey took one last look at the Big Chief notebook containing all his years of premonitions. Acting on a sudden impulse, he threw the notebook out the window. He didn't even look back as the wind opened the cover and sent the pages fluttering as the object drifted to the ground. For the first time in his life, he felt free.

The End

ABOUT THE AUTHORS

Dan Woll is a retired public school teacher, principal and superintendent. His world view is informed by a sink or swim rookie teaching experience in an inner city school, extensive mountaineering adventures, including an early technical ascent of El Capitan, and life in small town Wisconsin. He lives in River Falls, Wisconsin with his wife, Beth and his furry muse, Emmett, a Bernese Mountain Dog. Dan and Beth have three grown daughters. He is the author of *North of Highway 8*, *Further*, and co-author of *Death on Cache Lake*. He also collaborates with daughter Shelley on her children's *Sarah Saves* series.

Walter Rhein maintains a web page about travel, musings on writing, and other things at StreetsOfLima.com. His novels with Perseid Press include: *The Reader of Acheron*, *The Literate Thief*, and *Reckless Traveler*. His novel *The Bone Sword* is published with Harren Press, and his novel *Beyond Birkie Fever* was originally published with Rhemalda Publishing. He currently splits his time between the US and Peru, and can be reached for questions or comments at: WalterRhein@gmail.com.